Blood Tribute

VELA ROTH

FIVE THORNS PRESS

Blood Tribute

VELA ROTH

ISBN 978-1-957040-28-8 (Ebook)
ISBN 978-1-957040-29-5 (Paperback)

Edited by The Word Faery
thewordfaery.com

Cover illustration by Amira Naval
www.instagram.com/amiranaval

Cover design by GetCovers
www.getcovers.com

Formatting by Vela Roth

Published by Five Thorns Press
www.fivethorns.com

Visit www.velaroth.com

CONTENTS

Content Note v

One: A Profane Bargain 1

Two: The Circling Vulture 13

Three: The Immortal's Lair....................22

Four: A Sacred Kill 39

Five: The Forgotten Martyr....................51

Six: Unholy Confessions 61

Epilogue: Eternal Heresy 78

Preview: Blood Mercy............................86

CONTENT NOTE

For your self-care, content warnings can be found on the author's website at vroth.co/cw#tribute.

ONE

A Profane Bargain

NORA KNEW WHERE TO GO looking for the Hesperine—in the place where one of his kind had slaughtered her parents.

She hiked down through the woods with only the moons to light her way through the ghostly birch trees. She tried not to jump at shadows. Hesperines were always lurking in the darkness, yet impossible to detect. Until it was too late.

Seeking one out was a death wish. But what did she have to lose?

Nothing. Everything.

Her breath came faster, and the chill of oncoming autumn bit into her chest. The Hesperine would hear her heart pounding. He would smell her fear.

But the heretic wouldn't be able to sense the magic in her father's knightly dagger. The scabbard dug into her leg, securely hidden under her skirts. As long as she wielded Arceo, the Blade of Protection, the relic would keep the

Hesperine from manipulating her thoughts with his profane magic.

But he could still drink her blood.

She swallowed hard. It was the only way. Her plan depended on him sinking his fangs into her.

To strengthen her resolve, she glanced behind her at Castra Gloria, visible on a craggy rise above the golden treetops. Her beloved, decrepit fortress was all she had left. She could not lose it, too. She could not let her family's legacy end with her.

She was a woman, ineligible to become a holy knight. And incapable, it seemed, of fulfilling her most basic duty of securing one for a husband. There was only one way the Knightly Order of Andragathos would let her keep her inheritance. She, the last and least worthy of her line, must somehow prove herself worthy to be a dame in her own right.

By the gods, she would kill the Hesperine with her own hands. And she would survive it.

Nora faced the darkness and pushed forward.

When she came to the edge of the clearing, the familiar scene was a shock. Disjointed memories from six months before flashed through her mind. Her father's body falling. Her mother's scream. Her own blood…

Nora stood paralyzed for a moment that she could not afford to waste. She had barely survived that night. She must be braver if she didn't want to meet the same fate as her parents.

Her heart in her throat, she picked up her leaden feet and marched into the open. Brilliant fallen leaves crumbled beneath her footsteps. With a mundane knife, she cut her palm, biting back a hiss of pain.Nora held out her shaking, bleeding hand to make herself bait for the Hesperine.

Nothing happened. Moments passed as her blood dripped onto the ochre carpet of birch leaves. Treacherous relief slipped through her, chased by anger.

His kind had destroyed her family, but now he wouldn't deign to appear. Perhaps he, like everyone else, had deemed her unworthy.

How dare a reviled heretic dismiss her? She might be a failure as a lady and a daughter, but she would teach her enemy to take her seriously. Let him underestimate her. She would use that to her advantage, and the Hesperine would eat his words when she carved out his heart.

"I know you're here," she called out. "The least you can do is hear me out."

The wind swept gently through the spruces and mountain pines, as if mocking her.

She watched for any shadow that moved. "I know what you want, and I'll give it to you—willingly. If you meet my terms."

Hesperines were bestial, but cunning. With their preternatural strength and speed, they could easily take human blood by force. And yet, they preferred to use their powers of persuasion to ensnare willing victims. He would not be able to resist her offer, she was sure. She only hoped he wasn't in the mood to play with his prey.

When he appeared out of thin air in front of her, she jumped out of her skin.

He looked nothing like the illuminations in the sacred tomes. He was no snarling, creeping creature with corpse-like skin or long fangs dripping with blood.

His beard was neatly trimmed, her foolish brain noticed,

his complexion rich and dusky. He wore a short, elegant robe and trousers, not even stained with the gore of his last meal.

He looked…human.

Except he was far more beautiful than any mortal. Proud, dark brows, a chiseled jaw. The physique of a god. She couldn't stop staring at his full lower lip and the elegant bow of his upper one, expecting him to bear his fangs at any moment.

He held up his hands. "I didn't mean to frighten you."

His voice was deep, his accent musical, but with a guttural edge. He sounded so sincere, as if he wanted with all his heart to reassure her. He could whisper in a woman's ear and make her do anything he asked.

But not this woman.

"I am not afraid." She dropped her knife in the grass.

His gaze never strayed from hers. "Are you Nora?"

Her heart kicked against her ribs. How did he know the name only her family called her?

She lifted her chin and infused her voice with boldness she didn't feel. "I am Lady Honora of Gloria. Although my forefathers were dedicated to destroying your kind, I only want peace and safety for my people. I am prepared to negotiate a truce with you."

He lowered his hands slowly. "There is no need to negotiate. I've come to finish what my brother started."

"Your brother?"

"He was the Hesperine who was here that night."

She was looking at the brother of her parents' murderer. And he intended for her to be next.

But if she could turn the tables on him, justice would be

all the more poetic. She could avenge her parents and secure their legacy with one kill.

A hint of pain appeared on the Hesperine's face. "This… is the place where it happened, isn't it?"

He sounded vulnerable. Wounded. Did he expect her to fall for that?

"Yes," she answered, "this is the place where your brother ambushed my family on our way home. I watched him murder my parents. I would have died, too, if a Knight of Andragathos had not sent him fleeing with a fatal wound. But if you came here looking for revenge, you won't find it. I am prepared to let you leave alive, if you will do the same for me."

All trace of emotion left his expression. His stillness was far more frightening than his deceptive words. Now she saw the predator in him.

She envisioned how she would reach for her dagger if he sprang upon her. She had Arceo's protection. That kept her calm enough to say what she had rehearsed. She was a terrible liar, but now she must put on the best performance of her life to deceive a Hesperine.

"I will give you my blood for three nights as tribute," she said with dignity. "After that, you will leave, and no Hesperines will enter my lands again for as long as I hold Castra Gloria. Do you deem that a fair resolution to the bloodshed between our kin?"

He was silent for a long moment. Would he see through her promise and realize she was trying to trick him? Or would the temptation of her blood overrule his reason?

"I didn't come here for your blood," he said at last, his voice low and dangerous.

Her fury returned in full force. It was one matter for every eligible suitor in the Knightly Order of Andragathos to reject her. But for a bloodthirsty monster to stand here and tell her he didn't want her was a new low.

She thrust her hand out again, flexing it to bring forth more blood. "Isn't this enough for you? Would it not satisfy you to feed on the daughter of your enemies?"

His hands closed over hers before she could react. The controlled strength in his grasp made her knees go weak. He curled her fingers around the cut on her palm.

"Don't tempt me," he said.

So he was tempted. There was still hope her plan might work.

"Why refuse what is yours for the taking?" she asked. "I know you prefer the blood of the willing to feeding by force."

"You understand nothing."

"Enlighten me. If you have a different tribute in mind, tell me what you want."

He didn't release her hand. "I came for you."

Her mouth went dry. "If not my blood…then what do you want from me?"

He barely leaned toward her, but the space between them seemed to shrink to nothing. She found herself tilting her head back to look at him. His reflective eyes caught the moonlight and glowed gold. He didn't smell like blood and death. His scent was warm with spices and musky with masculine sweetness.

"I am here to take you away from the mortal world," he said. "Forever."

Her breath halted in her throat. Her carefully constructed

plan crumbled. What he wanted was so much worse than her blood.

"You want to turn me into one of you?" she breathed.

"You owe it to my brother."

She should have known a Hesperine would have a more twisted vengeance in mind. Not even her death would be enough for him. He wanted her, the last descendant of her devout line, to live forever as a heretic.

She yanked against his hold, scrambling away. He let her go so easily that she stumbled.

"I would never transform you by force," he said. "It seems I'll have to make you realize you want the Gift of immortality."

Oh, gods. He did intend to play with her.

"Give me your blood, as you offered," he demanded. "Then, if you still wish to banish Hesperines from your lands, we will never set foot here again. But if, after three nights with me, you cannot deny you want what I've shown you… you will let me transform you."

She had no trouble imagining what he planned to show her to change her mind.

"I am only offering you my blood." She hated how unsteady her voice was. "You will not take anything else. I want you to swear on your goddess."

"What does an oath in her name mean to you? Your people persecute us for worshiping her."

"Your kind are devoted enough to follow her into cursed eternity. Swearing by her means something to you."

"I will expect your oath in return."

"Very well. I, Lady Honora of Gloria, swear to give you

my blood for three nights, in the name of Andragathos, God of Virtue and patron of my line."

"I, Firstblood Daryavesh, swear by Hespera, Goddess of Night, that I will only take what you offer me willingly."

Deceptive Hesperine. That was not the promise she had asked of him. But the loophole he had left himself would win him nothing. Her blood was all he would get. She would die before she dishonored her parents' memory by offering a Hesperine her body.

Letting him bite her was defilement enough. But if she had to pay for her failures in blood, so be it.

"First, I will show you what the Drink is really like." He took a step forward.

On instinct, she backed up, only to trip against a boulder embedded in the grassy hillside. The Hesperine caught her and eased her down to sit on the stone.

She was about to sit here where her parents had been martyred and accept a heretic's bite.

Should she draw Arceo and try to end this now? Could she kill the Hesperine without letting him do this to her?

No, she was not foolish enough to try. She was neither a mage nor a warrior. She didn't stand a chance against the Hesperine unless she went through with her plan. She must survive his bite.

Three nights. Three doses of the Sunfire Poison in her blood. The knights applied the alchemical mixture to their blades, but without combat training, she must be creative. She had drunk the potion, turning herself into her weapon.

When Hesperines were slain, their bodies disappeared in a flash of light. To prove her deed to the Order, she would have to remove a trophy from him while he was still alive. After his third feeding, the poison would take effect, rendering him too slow and weak to fight her while she removed his heart.

She watched him uncurl her fingers, one by one. His nostrils flared, and his pupils expanded, turning his irises to gold rings.

He lifted her hand toward his mouth and licked her cut. It should have stung, but all she felt was the slow stroke of his tongue across her skin.

His hands tightened on hers, and if it was possible, he went even more still. As if held himself in check by a thread.

Before her eyes, her wound healed.

"What—?" she sputtered. "How?"

It seemed to take him a moment to find his voice. "A Hesperine's bite does no harm to a human. It has healing properties."

He swept his tongue over her palm again, licking away the blood that lingered on her skin.

She felt her cheeks heat and knew her hopelessly pale complexion turned a betraying shade of red. She always blushed too easily. She knew she was too expressive. It was one of her greatest flaws.

He pulled back, licking his sensual lips. Her first look at his fangs should have made her quail. But the sight of his unsheathed canines only made her face flush hotter. And the darkness wouldn't hide her response from his night vision.

It was not his strength and speed or even his magic that were the greatest threats to her. The true challenge would be surviving his seduction.

"This is what I will show you first, Nora. What the Drink

is really like. Then tell me if you still believe the knights' tales of horror." He rested her arm across her lap, wrist up, and pressed his fingers to her racing pulse.

She must not allow herself to forget how dangerous he was. But in that moment, she was not sure whom she feared more: him, or herself.

His mouth met her skin again, evoking a flare of sensation on her sensitive inner wrist. With her free hand, she clutched at the boulder to support herself. When he sucked gently, heat crept down her neck and across her breasts.

He paused. "The Drink is not an act of violence. It is a sacred ritual."

He firmed his grip on her forearm and held her wrist against his mouth. Her heart seemed ready to burst from her ribcage. There was no turning back now.

But no agony came. She felt the tips of his fangs prick her, then their hard lengths sinking into her flesh. But the sensation that spread through her body was anything but painful.

First a sparkling awareness that sent gooseflesh over her skin. Then a deeper warmth emanating from his lips and tongue. A sweet ache flowed down her arm, and she bit back a moan.

She knew he was pulling her lifeblood out of her, and yet the power of his bite seemed to pour into her as well, overwhelming. All the heat flowed to one destination, pooling low in her belly.

She had never let any male do this to her. She never gave in to such base desires, except in her solitary moments, when she banished her lust with her own hands. Her appetites had always been unbefitting a holy knight's daughter, but she had managed them. Until tonight.

How was this possible? Could he be using magic on her? She squeezed her thighs together. The scabbard strapped to her leg reminded her of the truth. This was no manipulation of her mind. This was all her.

With nothing more than a bite on her wrist, the Hesperine was undoing all her years of self control.

She tried to breathe through the flood of awareness coursing through her body. Her nipples pressed tight against the gown, and her nails dug into the stone. But she didn't push him off of her. She had to keep their agreement.

A voice in her mind, one she had tried to silence her whole life, whispered the truth to her. She didn't want him to stop.

He lay across her lap, his jaw taut, fastened to her wrist as if his next heartbeat depended on it. She felt the inexplicable urge to bury her fingers in his long black hair. Would he keep drinking until he drained all the life out of her? Would she let him?

Suddenly, he pulled his fangs out of her with a grunt of effort.

It was over. But no sigh of relief escaped her. She bit back a whimper of frustration.

He pressed his tongue to her wrist again. His licks knit her skin together and sealed his bite, leaving two pinpoints of exquisite sensitivity where his fangs had pierced her.

Suddenly he was standing out of arm's reach, so fast she didn't see him move. They stared at each other, their breaths loud in the quiet night.

No blood stained his lips. She stared at his fangs, still fully extended from his gums. Fangs that had just been in her flesh. She pressed a hand to her wrist, where those twin spots of sensation on her skin felt like an indelible mark.

"Tell me, Nora. Were the horror stories true?"

She said nothing. She wouldn't give him the satisfaction.

"Did it hurt?" he asked her.

Her hand tightened on her wrist, her core still throbbing.

"Remember our agreement," he said. "Can you deny that a Hesperine's bite is nothing like you imagined?"

She clenched her teeth. Two more nights. Then she could end their agreement with her blade.

"No," she confessed. "I cannot deny it."

Then he did the most dangerous thing of all. He smiled. That arrogant tilt of his mouth transformed his deadly expression into something far more devastating.

"Tomorrow night," he promised, "I'll show you more. Unless you're afraid for me to rob you of your assumptions."

She lifted her chin. "I will meet you here after sunset."

Assumptions were not all he intended to rob her of, she was sure. But their bargain would end with her maidenhead intact—and his heart on a platter.

TWO

The Circling Vulture

NORA STOOD BEFORE THE DOOR at the heart of the fortress. Sunlight speared down from the corridor's high windows, pinning her to the spot. She could not make herself take another step.

The morning after her tryst with a Hesperine, the last place she wanted to set foot was the shrine. The last person she wanted to see was Sir Virtus.

But she should not have been surprised the Knight Commander had come for a visit today. He always seemed to appear at precisely the moment to catch her in wrongdoing.

She wrenched her thoughts away from the Hesperine and the hours she had lain awake, her body burning with unfulfilled desire. Instead, she envisioned architectural diagrams. Her plans for the fortress expansion were so soothing.

Her calm splintered when she spotted a new crack in the wall between two tapestries. There could be no expansion until she managed the repairs.

The heavy old door groaned open, and she jumped. Sir Virtus stood in the doorway, his gold and white surcoat over-bright to her bleary eyes.

"Where is your mind, Honora?" He clucked his tongue, a frown on his patrician face. "Daydreaming about building palaces again?"

She made herself wait before replying, a lesson she had learned the hard way many times. The first words out of her mouth were always the wrong ones. Not that she ever said precisely the right thing.

"Uncle Virtus!" She was proud of the false cheer she managed to muster. "What brings you riding all the way up here? I wasn't expecting to see you until Autumn Equinox."

"Come." He held the door open and motioned her inside.

She broke out in a sweat, but pulled her shawl closer around her arms. If she hesitated, he would think she had something to confess. She forced her feet over the threshold.

The phantom pains flared along her arms, stinging her skin, aching much deeper within. She walked ahead of him so he wouldn't see her grimace.

The walls lined with relics seemed to shrink in on her, bringing the gleaming silver swords and chalices of holy fire dangerously close. The tomes chained to their stands seemed to judge her.

She carefully ignored the locked, inlaid box where only one of a pair of knightly daggers rested. Above all, she must not give him a reason to open the dagger case.

"Do not feign innocence, Honora." Sir Virtus's voice echoed through the shrine chamber.

Could he already know Arceo was missing? If he found

out she was hunting a Hesperine on her own, he would take the kill and the glory for himself. And if he found out she had let a Hesperine tarnish her with even one bite, he would subject her to purification.

She shut her eyes upon the shrine of Andragathos at the head of the room. But she could still see the white shield in her mind's eye. The god's glyph, emblazoned in golden spell light, seemed to burn through her eyelids.

Sir Virtus's footfalls halted beside her. "Did you think I wouldn't find out?"

She resisted the urge to cover her wrist with her hand.

"The news reached my ears," he said, "as soon as you failed to secure a proposal from your last suitor."

Slowly, Nora let out the breath she had been holding. She opened her eyes and looked up at him. "The Order gave me until Autumn Equinox to find a husband. I have two more days."

"My dear, we both know you have run out of unmarried knights to court you. Who else is there, and how could you manage to secure him in two days?"

She couldn't. But in that amount of time, she could poison and excardiate a Hesperine.

"You cannot build a palace in two days, either," Sir Virtus scoffed. "What is all the scaffolding in the corridors?"

"Some of the repairs cannot wait any longer. We've already had to put them off for too long, with skilled builders and materials in such short supply. Every noble house in Tenebra is scrambling to rebuild after the last round of feud sieges."

"What did I tell you about your improper preoccupation with architecture? The journals of your ancestors who built the fortress are entirely inappropriate reading material for a lady. If you devoted as much effort to weaving as you do to studying the fortifications, you would have found a husband by now."

She knew her obsession with the fortress was one of her weaknesses. But at least it was a useful one that kept Castra Gloria from falling down around their ears. She made certain not to babble about it to her suitors. Not that it had mattered.

Sir Virtus sighed. "You must understand the Order's stipulation. Castra Gloria was granted to your distant forefather in recognition of his deeds, but his heirs were entitled to hold it only as long as they continued to supply knights or wives to the Order."

She bit her tongue and waited out his lecture.

"If only I were your uncle by blood, so we could keep the fortress in the family. But your father was my brother-in-arms. In his absence, it is my sacred duty to guide you. I have done my best, but you are already twenty-four, and we all know you lack the forbearance and modesty to be a holy knight's lady. It is time to accept that you will never marry."

How dare he? He was not her father. And she was not a fool. She knew who stood to gain the most if Castra Gloria reverted to the Order's possession.

Sir Virtus lived and breathed for the Order—and for his position in it. Her family's relics and strategic keep would bring power and prestige to the holy knights and thus, to Sir Virtus.

Nora had always suspected he envied her father's accomplishments. The way he had been circling like a vulture since her parents' deaths only confirmed it. He already acted like he lived here, arriving whenever he pleased, ordering her servants about as if he was their master.

Without invitation, he knelt in the place where her father had always prayed. "The other knights will arrive on Autumn Equinox to rededicate the fortress to the Order. But do not fear for your future, my dear. You know I will always watch over you. You can come to live in my stronghold, under my guidance."

For once, Nora didn't have to fight to hold in an unwise outburst. Her throat closed. The air left her lungs. She huddled in her shawl, the phantom pains slashing over her skin.

This was the future he envisioned for her. Her family legacy would end with an embarrassment the Order preferred to forget. She would lose her good name, her home, and any shred of power she had over her own fate. She would exist under his watchful eye for the rest of her life.

Sir Virtus had saved her from the Hesperine who had murdered her parents. She might owe him her life, but not her obedience. Her home. Her legacy.

She would have to carry out the rest of her plan under his nose. She knew what a desperate idea it was. There had only been a handful of dames in the history of the Order. But despite her shortcomings, she would make her parents proud. Even if they were not here to see it.

She would hold her castle.

Nora crept along the corridor, keeping to the shadows between the torches. Her scaffolding lay in piles of dismantled timbers. How quickly Lord Virtus had ordered it taken down. How willingly the servants who had known her all her life had hastened to obey him.

At the open doorway to the shrine, she pressed against the wall, staying clear of the light that spilled out. Paper rustled. Sir Virtus was still awake, helping himself to her family's books? She had thought he would be abed by now.

She crossed to the far side of the corridor where the glow didn't quite reach, but the shadows were not deep enough. Her heart pounding, she ducked behind the remains of the scaffolds. One stride. Two. Three.

She was past the open doorway. She straightened, slipping into the gloom, and breathed a sigh of relief.

Then a hand closed over her shoulder.

She swallowed a shriek, halting in her tracks. The hand spun her around. She looked up into the shadowed face of Sir Virtus.

"Honora." His low, quiet rebuke sent a chill down her spine. "What is a holy knight's daughter doing out of her chambers at this unholy hour?"

Nora knew she wore her guilt and anger on her face for him to see. Hiding her reactions was not a skill she possessed. Her only hope was to construct a lie that matched her expression.

"I came to check on the repairs. I knew you would disapprove, so I waited until after dark. How could you take down the scaffolding, Uncle Virtus?"

He made a derisive sound. "Get your head out of your diagrams, girl. Imagine what people will think if you wander the halls at night, as if out for a tryst!"

"Of course, Uncle Virtus. I'll go straight back to bed."

She ducked out of his hold and turned back the way she had come.

He caught one of her arms in a tight grip. She bit back a cry of pain. Dragging her a step closer to him, he loomed over her in the half-light.

"Is scaffolding all you have been playing with, Honora?" He squeezed her arm harder.

She blinked back tears. "What can you mean?"

"Arceo is missing from the shrine. Sancti is alone in the dagger case."

Sancti, the Blade of Purification. The relic's name sent a pall over her. If Sir Virtus had opened the dagger case, he was planning to use Arceo's twin.

Sir Virtus leaned nearer. "Are architecture journals all you've been playing with, Nora?"

She shrank back. "You know I would never go near the dagger case."

"Must I remind you how valuable those relics are?" His voice rose. "Your father was the youngest knight to receive the honor of carrying Sancti. It brought him glory all the years he possessed it. And when they finally conveyed Arceo upon him as well, it was the crowning achievement of his service to the Order."

If only they had known a Hesperine would be waiting to ambush him on the way home from the ceremony. If only the relics had been enough to save her parents.

"You don't have to remind me," Nora said. "My father died for Arceo."

"Yes, he did. And like everything else in this castle, the daggers belong to the Order now. Do you understand me?"

She dropped her gaze. "Yes, Uncle Virtus."

"You know how forgiving I am," he said more quietly. "I will take no action until after dawn rites. That will give you the opportunity to confess, if there is anything you're hiding from me. But if Arceo is not in the case by the end of my morning prayers, there will be consequences."

"One of the servants must have stolen it." Nora had no qualms about blaming the traitors. "We can start searching the castle after dawn rites."

"You'd best hope we find it among the servants, then."

The relic would be safe in the one place ascetic Sir Virtus would never look. Up a virgin's skirts.

"Get back to your rooms." He shoved her away from him and watched her flee.

When she was certain he hadn't followed her, she cut down a side passage, then slipped through a hidden archway behind a tapestry. She knew every twist and turn of Castra Gloria that had been built, rebuilt, and cobbled together over the centuries.

The moons were high in the sky by the time she reached the clearing. The moment she stepped out of the trees, the Hesperine appeared.

"I began to think you had reconsidered our agreement," he said.

"I was merely delayed." She straightened, trying to catch her breath. "I keep my oaths, Firstblood Dar—Dayr…"

He arched a brow at her. "If you find my full name too difficult to pronounce, you may call me Dav."

She cleared her throat. "Well, that only seems fair, since you refuse to call me by my proper name."

"Yes I do…Nora." Her name sounded indecent on his tongue. "I have many things to show you tonight."

Curse her heart, already starting to pound. His pupils expanded, and his lips parted, giving her a glimpse of his fangs.

"Not that sort of demonstration," he said. "I intend to teach you about Hesperine culture."

She frowned at him. "I am not here for a lesson in heresy. Take my blood and be done with it."

"Ah, but I have my side of the agreement to keep as well." He held out his hand to her. "Come with me."

She shrank back. "Where do you intend to take me?"

The corner of his mouth twitched. "To my lair."

She stood rooted to the spot. "You have a lair? On my lands?"

"Yes, but you cannot get in unless I take you there."

"This is not part of our agreement."

"Our agreement did not place any limitations on where your tribute will take place."

"You cannot expect me to abscond with you."

His gaze dropped to the grass. "I will not continue drinking from you in this place."

Silence fell between them. If he had tried to trick or cajole her, she would have dug her heels in. But she could not, in truth, fault him for this. Neither of them wanted their next battle to take place here where their kin had died.

She had already placed herself at his mercy. What matter if she went deeper into danger with him?

She took his hand.

THREE

The Immortal's Lair

THIS WOMAN WAS THE REASON Dav's brother was dead. She had no right to smell like life itself.

When she slid her hand in his, he fought the urge to pull her closer. His eyes focused on her wrist, and his fangs unsheathed at the memory of her skin giving way to his bite. The mere scent of her blood was enough to make him forget where they were.

He could not afford to forget. His brother's life, which should have been eternal, had been cut short. Here. For the sake of this mortal's fleeting existence.

Dav must never lose sight of this—Nora's blood was a means to an end.

He took a step back, and with it, stepped away from the clearing with her. His effortless magic seemed to leave her reeling. She peered at their new surroundings, swaying on her feet, and stumbled into him.

As her body made contact with his, Dav cursed inwardly.

He had forgotten that stepping with a Hesperine was uncomfortable for mortals who were not adjusted to it.

He'd also forgotten how long it had been since he'd held a female this close. Nora was bundled up in layers of wool and propriety, and yet the feeling of her leaning into him made his whole body tighten.

Grief was a twisted master. For months, it had isolated Dav. Now it threw Nora into his arms.

He set her on her feet and strode away, putting the table between them. She tracked him with her gaze, her brown eyes wary, as if he were a predator that might pounce.

"Does this look like a beast's den?" he asked her.

She took in the warm spell lights, the paper and ink arranged on the table, the tidy scroll racks along the wall. The round chamber was all that remained of an ancient tower, but at least it was hospitable, for a ruin.

"Where are we?" she asked.

"A Hesperine Sanctuary. The spells over this place protect it from discovery and destruction. Your Order will never be able to find it."

"Good. I don't want them interfering with our agreement."

She seemed to decide he was not about to make a human sacrifice of her at quill point. She roamed over to one of the arched windows. Her candid face lit up, and her aura shone, an unseen light he could feel with his arcane senses.

The Blood Union revealed all mortal emotions to Hesperines. It was, perhaps, their greatest magical ability…and greatest weakness. For five hundred years, Dav had vicariously experienced every shade of human experience, from joy to despair. And yet none of their emotions had sunk so deep into his veins as hers.

Her wonder glittered through him, a mockery of his own pain, and he wanted to claw her feelings out from under his skin.

She smiled, drawing his attention to her generous mouth. "This is the architectural style of the Great Temple Epoch! The structure must be at least fifteen centuries old."

"I'm not that familiar with your history." Nothing in the kingdom of Tenebra had ever mattered to Dav. Until his brother had met his fate here.

Nora scarcely seemed to notice the rose vines that spilled through the window frame from outside. She ran her hand along the stonework. A thorn tore her skin, painting one of her fingertips red. The fragrance of her blood bloomed in the air.

Dav took a Hesperine step, transporting himself to her side. He had pulled her hand halfway to his mouth before he realized what he was doing.

They both froze. Blood dripped from her finger onto one white rose. His mouth went dry, parched for his next taste of her.

By the Goddess, he was an educated, intelligent immortal who never struggled with self control. He would not let any human reduce him to this, least of all her.

Slowly, he released her, to prove to himself that he could.

She scuttled away from the roses, cradling her bleeding hand. "Are those Harlot's Kiss?"

He huffed. "That's what you call roses here, isn't it? I suppose you've never seen one in person."

She swallowed. "Tenebrans set fire to them wherever they spring up."

He nearly rolled his eyes. "Yes, they are Hespera's sacred

flower. No, pricking your finger on one will not destroy your soul or any of that other nonsense."

"But they have magical properties associated with your goddess."

"Nothing that will harm you." He turned his back on her and crossed the room. He was not fleeing from the temptation of her blood. He was exhibiting self-mastery.

His fangs throbbed, taunting him.

"We are not animals, Nora. We are scientists, artists…" He gestured around them. "Architects."

Curiosity sparked in her aura. Apparently, the way to Nora's heart was through historical buildings. Dav had never thought a window arch would prove the key to his plan, but if this was an opening he could use, he would take it.

He beckoned her over to one of the walls, where a bas relief was overgrown with rose vines. With a touch of magic, he swept the blooms aside to reveal the red stone beneath. The carving depicted Hespera as a beautiful woman clothed only in her flowing hair.

Nora gasped and stared for a speechless moment. "This has to be a portrayal of Hespera from before worship of her was outlawed. Most of the carvings from this era were destroyed in the Last War. This is exquisitely preserved."

His empathic abilities tortured him with every flavor of her emotions. Her fascination with the architecture was more powerful than her disapproval of his goddess.

Dav said, "This ruin is just a small example of our architecture. There are glorious cities in Orthros built in styles you've never seen before."

At the mention of the Hesperine homeland, a shudder

went through her. "I suppose you would need buildings, even in the Land of Eternal Night."

"It isn't a frozen wasteland of death and destruction. It is a place of great beauty and sophistication, a pinnacle of learning and the arts."

She scowled at him. "Your fangs weren't made for sipping fine wine. You expect me to believe you sit about painting and reading whenever you aren't invading my lands and dragging me into your lair?"

For the last seven months, Dav had sat about watching his entire life collapse. Until Queen Soteira had told him that the only way for him to finish grieving was to finish his brother's mission. She, his gentle mentor, had tossed him out on his arse and told him to go to Tenebra.

"I'm a mind healer by profession," he said.

You were. The voice of doubt had followed him here. *What kind of healer cannot mend himself?*

Nora tensed. "You're a mind mage?"

"No. Not a mind mage, a mind *healer.* My magic cannot manipulate your thoughts, only restore them to what they should be. It's the same principle as a healer mage mending a broken leg, except I work on broken minds. My power can repair the inner damage from harmful spells or painful life experiences."

Where is your power now? the voice taunted.

As he so often had in the past half year, Dav reached within himself on reflex, deep into the well where his mind healing magic had always dwelt. And once again, he found only emptiness.

He, one of the most powerful theramancers in Orthros,

could no longer wield a drop of his own magic. He was a wreck held together by the innate Hesperine abilities he could still use.

Queen Soteira said magic couldn't die. But Dav had felt no sign of life from his power since his brother had died in his arms.

Nora's scent sharpened with anxiety. "I've never heard of such magic before."

This was what Dav hated to sense most of all. Her fear clawing at the Blood Union. Bleeding thorns, he was a healer. Not a monster.

Aren't you? the voice whispered. *You want her pain. You want her remorse. You want her to atone until she breaks the way you have.*

He tried to keep his tone calm, factual. "Mind healing is not practiced in Tenebra, but it is an honorable calling in Orthros. So you see, Hesperines have better things to do than roam around your kingdom stalking humans."

If only his brother had stayed in the safety of their queendom, instead of venturing into these dangerous mortal lands.

Nora's righteous fury blazed through Dav's senses, colliding in chaos with his own. "Then why did your brother come here and take my parents from me? Why did he almost kill me?"

That accusation again. After everything Dav's brother had suffered because of her. How dare she say this of Rahim, the kindest soul Dav had ever known?

Rahim had always believed the best of people. He had been the one with compassion for Tenebrans. And it had gotten him killed because of this ungrateful mortal.

Dav didn't know if Nora was trying to deceive him

about that night for her own ends, or if she truly believed her warped version of events. But he had two more chances to find out what game she was playing.

He would strip away the lies, one by one, until he laid her bare.

"By the time our agreement comes to an end," he said, "you will understand."

She thrust out her hand. "Get on with it, then."

He didn't take her offering. "Tonight, I will show you I can be trusted with more than your wrist. Will you offer me your throat?"

Her face flushed. Goddess help him, it was so easy to make her blush. He wouldn't have needed the Blood Union to read her response to him. But the warmth of her anger and attraction washed over his Hesperine senses as well.

"You're sweating, Nora. Will you let me take your cloak?"

She clutched it closer about her for an instant, but then slowly unfastened it and handed it to him. He tossed it away onto the nearby cot. She rigidly ignored the bed.

She needn't have worried. She was the last person he had any intention of bedding. It was hardship enough that their agreement required him to drink her blood.

Oh, indeed, what a hardship. The voice of doubt had become the call of temptation.

No, Dav was not doing this for himself. This was for his brother.

Rahim's last wish had been for Dav to turn Nora into a Hesperine. He would do whatever he must to convince her to go through with it.

What better way to prove her wrong about Hesperines

than this? Her beliefs about his kind, her family, and herself would not survive three bites from him.

He would destroy her assumptions with his fangs, and he would taste her confession in her blood.

Not such a sacred act now, is it? taunted his darker self.

She wasn't making it easy for him. Her gray mourning gown covered her from neck to ankles, and a scarf shrouded her head and throat.

"Will you unwrap your scarf for me?" he asked.

"It's immodest for a woman to uncover her hair before a man who isn't her husband."

"I'm not a man. I'm a Hesperine." He drew nearer. "And giving me your blood last night was far more immodest than showing me your hair."

She bit her lip. What would that lip taste like? What would her teeth feel like biting him? He shut the thoughts away, but he could not ignore the snap of arousal in her scent or the blaze of her aura. Unruly, undimmable. Vital.

"Do you enjoy things you've been told are wrong, Nora?"

Her eyes flashed, and she snarled, "I am doing this for Gloria. Not myself. Don't you dare forget it."

She tore off the scarf and threw it on the ground. Her hair tumbled free, falling to her waist in wild red curls. Dav stopped breathing.

The scarf crumpled under his heel as he slipped behind her. She froze. When he lifted his hand, she didn't shy away.

He wrapped one ginger curl around his finger. "What else are you hiding under your holy principles?"

"Things you cannot take from me, no matter what you do to me."

"I will only take what you offer," he reminded her. "You have nothing to fear from me."

Are you not her worst fear?

He pulled the heavy curtain of her hair away from her neck. Letting its soft weight slide through his hands, he laid it over her other shoulder to leave her throat bare. He traced his fingertips along the sensitive juncture of her neck and shoulder and felt a shiver dance across her skin.

"Will you offer me your throat?" he asked.

"Yes." The word came out in a husky whisper.

He covered her hand with his and pressed her palm amid the roses, bracing them against the marble carvings. A quiver of excitement went through her.

He buried his other hand in the tangle of her hair, tilting her head. The flow of her blood called to his arcane senses, a coppery pulse summoning his fangs. His canines ached, but he made himself wait.

He was in control. But she was not, judging by her racing heartbeat.

"Can you deny you want me to bite your throat?" he murmured.

"I'm offering it to you freely. Isn't that enough for you?"

"No." He lowered his head and kissed her neck.

He could taste the musk of her arousal on her skin. His deprived body rose to attention in the confines of his trousers. Goddess, why did this woman seem perfectly crafted to torture him?

"Admit it, Nora. You want my bite."

"I have agreed to it."

"You want it," he ground out.

He closed his mouth over her vein and sucked her skin. His reward was a strangled little whimper from her. What would such an expressive woman sound like when she climaxed? Dav would wager a Hesperine could make her scream, and not from fright.

This time, he gave her no gentle bite. He took her vein fast and hard. She cried out, an unmistakable sound of pleasure. Her blood flowed warm and thick into his mouth, rich with the flavor of her lust. His own blood seemed to halt in his veins and wrench in a new direction. His thoughts faded, and his body hardened.

He was still in control, he told himself. But she was on the brink of falling from her self-righteous pedestal. He pulled back, her blood trailing warm and wet down his chin. His lips left a crimson smear on her pale skin as he spoke in her ear. "Can you deny you like how my fangs feel inside you?"

"You can't read my thoughts," she accused.

"I don't need to. I can taste it in you. You want me to bite you again, don't you?"

"Yes," she hissed.

He sank his fangs into her once more. Her hand came to his face. But she didn't push him away. Her fingers dug into his scalp, holding him to her vein with a vengeance.

His jaw locked, and he swallowed her lifeblood. She was so alive. Rahim was dead. Dav begrudged Nora each beat of her heart. But he drank down every surge of the elixir that heart pumped for him. He didn't want her here, weaving into his blood. But his own heart pounded harder, driving her essence into the cold reaches of his veins and filling him with her warmth.

He tightened his bite, tugging on her hair. Her head fell back against his shoulder. Her shapeless gown could not disguise the fullness of her breasts or the way her chest rose and fell with a harsh sigh of pleasure. A savage desire overtook him to unbind the rest of her as he had her hair.

He slid his hand down to grip the column of her throat. Her pulse pattered faster under his touch. He slipped his fangs out of her neck and nipped her earlobe. "Can you deny that blush of yours goes all the way to your breasts?"

Her hand curled into a fist upon the wall. "My blood is all you'll get from me."

"You've already given me more than that. You didn't promise me the flavor of your desire in the bargain."

"Go to Hypnos."

"Holy knights' daughters aren't supposed to swear by the god of death, either. But no one can hear you except a heretic. No one will ever know if you ask me to give you what you want."

He drove his fangs back into her slowly. A moan escaped her. He began to suckle her, pleasuring her vein, teasing each sip out of her and onto his tongue. Her breath came faster.

Her hand slipped from his hair, coming to rest on his where he held her throat. Her nails dug into his hand, prying him off of her. Tugging his hand down to the laces on the front of her gown.

He took over, teasing apart her laces one by one. She whimpered in frustration. He went slower. She cursed him again, but yanked the loose portion of her bodice out of his way.

When her gown hung open to her belly, another layer of fabric got in his way. Finding another lace at her collar, he loosened the wide neck of her undergarment and pulled the fabric down.

A thick band of cloth wrapped around her chest, viciously tight. Dav felt an unexpected rush of anger at the binding that held her natural figure in a vise. With a whip of levitation, he tore it off of her. She gasped as her breasts swung free.

He could make an entire banquet off of them after he was done with her blood. He swept his forearm under the heavy globes, pressing them up toward him. Just as he'd imagined, a rosy flush swept all the way down to her taut nipples.

She shifted her head to look down at what he was doing to her. The motion tugged against his fangs, sending a jolt of pleasure through him. He wrapped his hand around one breast and massaged her, and there came an echoing jolt of pleasure in her aura.

Her whole body tensed, as if she were fighting to hold still. He kept kneading and teasing her breasts, dragging at her vein. Her fist uncurled, and she flattened her hand on the wall. He pressed his fingers between hers, trapping her.

Her blood escaped his lips, trickling down past her collarbone, over the swell of her breast. He caught the crimson trail on his fingers. When he swept the warm liquid over her nipple, the peak drew tighter. He played with the tight bud between his slippery fingers.

She arched back against him, pressing into his straining trousers. Through her thick skirts, he felt an impression of wide hips and full buttocks. The foretaste of her release enriched her blood and filled him with a sense of triumph.

He would not bed her. But he would make her climax against this wall.

He suckled her relentlessly, giving her breasts no mercy from his hand. Her divine pleas dissolved in wordless mewls. Her free hand struck the wall, seeking purchase.

At last, her shocked outcry echoed through the chamber. She came apart, grinding back against him, a wanton mirror of his goddess. He tasted her prim self-control explode into pure, carnal defiance.

He had thought he knew the flavor of a woman's ecstasy, but no lover of his had ever tasted like this. He shouted against her throat, his body pounding with vicarious pleasure, aching in the grip of his own hunger.

When the crest of her release faded from her blood, and her body calmed, she still rubbed softly back against him, panting.

He gave her neck a long lick. "That barely took the edge off, did it?"

"Oh, *gods*," she uttered.

"Only Hespera can hear your prayers." He braced his feet, nudging the ridge of his erection in the gentle groove he could feel through her skirts. "Do you know why Hesperines prefer willing humans?"

She canted her hips, exploring how they fit together. "Because you're manipulative bastards, that's why."

"Because free Will is sacred to Hespera. We never violate a mortal's power of choice. This is up to you. If you want more, you must ask for it."

Her curious movements were a guileless, wicked tease.

"Is this an offer?" he gritted.

She stilled, trembling. He sensed a battle raging in her, an old one that had always been tearing her apart.

It ended in surrender. She leaned forward against the wall and stretched her back, offering her hips into his waiting hands.

"Ask me, Nora."

He heard her swallow. Then her whisper. "Take my body, too."

He would not bed her. He would thrust inside her right here.

He leaned his weight into her, pressing her closer to the wall. He wanted to sample a different side of her neck as he discovered just how wet his first drink had left her. Sweeping her hair to her other shoulder, he yanked the layers of her clothes down to her elbows, trapping her arms at her sides.

His gaze arrested on her arms. Scars criss-crossed her skin, some old, some new, a long history of pain written on her skin in long slashes. The most recent chapter was a set of new bruises, angry red imprints in the shape of a man's fingers.

Dav wanted to break his oaths as a healer. He wanted to snap this man's hand one finger at a time and listen to them crack.

With the utmost care, Dav brushed his fingertips over the angry marks on Nora's skin. She flinched, and he felt her past fear in the Blood Union.

Then memories flashed across the surface of her thoughts, as clear to Dav as if she had described them. A brutal hand. A threatening voice. Her inner wounds cried out to him.

For the first time in half a year, his magic stirred within him. His sleeping power soared to life and revealed the depths of Nora's mind.

Her inner world was a landscape of scars. They were small,

a thousand little cuts. But over the short years of her mortal existence, they had disfigured her inside.

At her center lay an ugly injury that had never healed. He recognized the bends and breaks in her thoughts. No natural experience, however traumatic, could have caused this. A spell had invaded the Sanctuary of her inmost self to twist and shatter her memories.

She hadn't been lying. It wasn't her fault that she didn't know the truth about Rahim's death. She didn't even remember that night.

Dav took a step back, his body throbbing with cooling lust and unspeakable rage. Nora's tormentor had committed the unforgivable act—violating a person's Will.

He bared his fangs. "Who did this to you?"

She pulled her gown up over her arms. "No one who concerns you."

"Tell me who he is."

"Why does it matter? Am I not human chattel to you?"

He rested his hands on her shoulders and eased her around to face him. She clutched her hair, pulling it across her chest to cover herself.

"Did I make you feel like chattel tonight?" he asked.

Her gaze dropped to her feet. Memories of his mouth and hands flitted through her mind, and the scars there twisted her pleasure into shame.

He wanted to worship her against this wall until she regretted nothing.

But she snapped, "You've had your second tribute. Take me home."

Dav cupped her cheek, lifting her face toward him. She

looked more startled at the gentle touch than at her first glimpse of his fangs.

"Who. Is. He."

Her eyes narrowed. "I suppose you want to make sure no one snatches your human plaything from you before you're done with me. Very well. I don't fancy the Order killing you before we complete our bargain, either. I should warn you that Sir Virtus has moved himself into my castle. Be careful. He's a Knight Commander in the Order of Andragathos."

The pieces fell into place. Sir Virtus was the man who had wounded Nora—and the knight who had dealt Rahim his death wound.

For the first time in his existence, Dav wanted to feel another's suffering in the Blood Union. That empathy was what prevented Hesperines from abusing their great power. Awareness of others' pain stayed them from causing it. But Dav would enjoy Sir Virtus's pain.

His reborn magic felt raw, achingly aware of Nora's thoughts. He tried to apply his power as he had done with his patients, to follow the pathways of pain through her thoughts to answers that could heal her. But his magic ebbed, then surged, slipping from his control. It was alive and well, but he felt like an apprentice relearning how to be a mage.

Dav wracked his own memory for his scant knowledge of Tenebra, now regretting the years he'd spent in his ivory tower. How could a Knight of Andragathos have caused these wounds in her mind? "Do I recall correctly that the holy knights do not possess magic of their own?"

"Right. Anyone with magic is required to enter a temple and become a mage instead of a warrior."

"But your Order fights with enchanted weapons."

"They pledge themselves to our god, so they're the only warriors permitted to wield magical artifacts. Sir Virtus has access to relics that can harm a Hesperine and the training to use them."

"Will you be safe from him during the day?" Dav silently cursed the sun. He would soon be locked in the Dawn Slumber, unable to wake until night returned.

"I can protect myself."

"Are you certain Sir Virtus will not harm you while I Slumber?" Dav pressed.

"He is the one at a disadvantage. It's my castle." She turned her back on Dav, lacing up her bodice. "You can take me back to the clearing now. When you meet me there tomorrow night, be careful."

"No," he said, "tomorrow, I will come to you."

"What? That's madness. You mustn't, not while Sir Virtus is there." She rounded on him.

Dav gave in to the urge to run his hand over her riot of curls. Her breath caught in her throat.

"I don't want him to catch you sneaking out," Dav said.

She pressed her lips together, but did not disagree. "The fortress is riddled with relics that can alert him to a Hesperine's presence, though."

"Can you clear one room and wait for me there?"

Nora swallowed. "Very well. Tomorrow night…come to my bedchamber."

FOUR

A Sacred Kill

Nora would make the Hesperine pay for every sound of pleasure he had dragged out of her with his unholy hands.

She fastened her scabbard, then straightened her gold and white festival gown. She'd been wearing this at the ceremony when the Order had bestowed Arceo upon her father. And when Dav's brother had killed her parents before her eyes.

Tonight, she would not forget who she was.

She threw back the blankets on the ancestral bed. The lady of Gloria's chamber was her rightful place, and she would dedicate tonight's kill to the righteous women of her line. She was hardly the first who'd had her bedchamber invaded by a Hesperine. It was on record that one noble widow had slain her would-be seducer and been elevated to dame for her feat.

Nora stoked the fire, the element that was every Hesperine's nemesis. Her poker was in easy reach, as were the torches she had placed in brackets around the room. Her chamber was devoid of Hesperine-detecting relics and full of extra weapons she could rely on if anything went wrong.

She had almost failed last night. She had come within an inch of giving herself to that creature.

But tonight, she was ready. She would slay not only her family's enemy, but her personal monster.

His presence seemed to fill the room, then he melted out of the shadows beyond the glow of the hearth. "Did Sir Virtus try anything during the day?"

"He still has no idea you're here."

Dav's nostrils flared. He stalked toward her, his expression dangerous. Nora's heart jumped, but she stood her ground.

His fangs flashed as he spoke. "He harmed you again."

"That is none of your affair. I am here for the tribute, aren't I?"

The firelight played across Dav's tawny skin, and in its wild light, she could almost imagine his face softened. "Nora, I can smell that you're still bleeding. I could heal that for you as I did the cut on your hand."

"*No.*" She retreated toward the fire, covering her upper arm with her hand. "Ask for my throat again. Or we can negotiate other places where you may take the tribute. But keep away from my arms."

To her astonishment, he offered her a bow. "Understood. I will respect that at all times."

She hesitated, her whole body humming with tension.

"Your arms are not up for debate," he said.

She eased toward him again. "Then where do you intend to drink from me tonight?"

"There's something I'd like to show you first." He gestured

to the scroll under his arm. "You have my word that it contains no harmful magic. It's a history text I ran across in the tower. Another Hesperine left it behind, perhaps as a gift for the next homesick wanderer."

So more heresy lessons were what he had in mind. Well, a history text didn't sound seductive in the least. If it would give her a reprieve from his other means of persuasion, she would go along with this.

She crossed to her worktable and shuffled her clutter to clear a space in the chaos. "Put it here then."

He joined her, his gaze falling to her drawings. Suddenly she regretted not hiding them before he had come. Having his eyes on her diagrams made her feel naked in a way even last night's transgressions had not.

"Is this your work?" he asked.

"Yes." No use in denying it. Her obsession earned her enough scorn from mortals. She could withstand some mockery from a Hesperine.

The censure and everything else would disappear the next time she picked up her quill. It was so easy to get lost in her work for hours, utterly focused on measurements and materials, unaware of the world around her.

"Your mathematics are so precise." He tilted his head, studying her plan for a new tower. "And your illustrations are beautiful."

She started gathering up her sketches. Let him use anything else to flatter his way into her bed. Not this.

"I am no expert," he said, "but these are very impressive to me. Are there any options for women to become professional architects in Tenebra?"

"Ha, ha." She rolled up the large sheets of parchment and stowed them under the table.

He unrolled his scroll. "This is an illustration of one of Orthros's cities."

Nora stood back, not looking at the page. "I have seen the Order's illustrations of your den, thank you."

Dav arched a brow. "How can those portrayals be accurate? Have any of the knights ever been there?"

"No, because no Tenebran who goes to Orthros ever returns to tell the tale."

"That's because they prefer to stay." He gestured to the open scroll. "Is it hard to understand why?"

If Nora's convictions could not survive the temptation of one architecture illustration, it did not bode well for her efforts to resist his touch later. She went forward and looked at his godsforsaken drawing.

Her expectations crumbled. The exquisite painting portrayed a city of palaces topped with majestic domes. Pointed arches graced covered portals with vaulted, honeycombed ceilings, and vibrant mosaics adorned every surface. She could never have imagined the elaborate designs in her wildest dreams…but someone had.

She didn't know if she believed this could be a real place, but even if it weren't, this beautiful dream had come from a Hesperine's mind and hands.

"This city was designed by Firstblood Yasamin," Dav said. "She is one of our greatest architects, the founder of the Yasamini movement."

"She invented her own architectural style?" All of this… had come from a *woman's* mind.

Was he lying? Most likely not. Hesperines worshiped a goddess and let females fornicate with whomever they pleased. Why not let them be architects, too?

"This is my favorite city in the world," Dav said. "The architecture draws inspiration from the human land where both Yasamin and I began our mortal lives. Granted, she is a thousand years older than me."

That finally tore Nora's gaze away from the unfairly beautiful illustration. For the first time, she looked into Dav's ethereal face and tried to see the human he had once been. "You say Hesperines don't force humans to transform. Does that mean you chose this life?"

"Yes." A shadow passed over his expression. "My brother and I came from a family of physicians in the Empire. I specialized in mind healing and he in physical healing. After my service in the Imperial Army treating soldiers' mental wounds, I…needed a change. We went to Orthros together to study with the Hesperines and decided to stay."

"The Empire?" She gaped.

He caught hold of her fingers, and the sudden touch sent a little shock through her. He spread her pale hand out upon his broad, brown one. "Couldn't you tell?"

"I assumed you were from Cordium, to the south of here."

He huffed. "Do I seem like a pompous, superstitious cleric from the Magelands?"

"N-no." The smooth warmth of his skin reminded her how his hand had felt elsewhere. Oh gods, why couldn't he have felt cold and clammy, as Hesperines were supposed to? "I've heard of the Empire across the sea, but I thought it was only a tale."

He gave her a bemused look. "It was quite real when I visited last year. The Empire has an alliance with Orthros, and people travel freely between for trade and education."

"So you chose to become a heretic so you could…study?"

"Can't fathom me giving up my soul for my books, can you?"

"Surely there was something in your mortal life you wanted to stay for."

"My time as a human taught me that no matter how much we learn about the mind, it is still the most mysterious frontier of exploration. It will take us Hesperine lifetimes to learn how to truly heal such a complex part of ourselves. I want to be a part of that research. Don't you think it would take you centuries to learn everything there is to know about every architectural style in the world?"

She pulled her hand away.

Dav brushed his fingers across her temple. "Imagine. You could study with Yasamin herself and be admired for your expertise in architecture."

Nora's chest ached.

He tugged at a curl that was trying to escape her hair veil. "You could design and construct your own monuments that would stand for centuries. Generations of students would know your name."

In that moment, she hated the Hesperines more than she ever had.

The curl sprang free, and Dav ran the tendril of her hair through his fingers. "Imagine if you could sit for hours, dreaming up your next project and sketching construction plans, with no one to interrupt or reprove you."

Immortality…power…none of those things tempted her. But this?

What a fool she was, to think of giving up her soul for such a simple thing.

"Imagine…" he began.

She couldn't bear to hear any more. Somehow, she had to silence his alluring voice, put a stop to these words so perfectly aimed at her heart.

He lowered his head toward her to murmur in her ear. "Imagine a male who finds your fixation on architecture one of the most beautiful things about y—"

She cut him off by covering his treacherous mouth with her own. She held his face in her hands and punished him for his words with her kiss.

He leaned into the rough strokes of her lips, his beard scraping her chin. Then he opened for her, and she fell, invading his mouth before she could catch herself.

Their tongues clashed, and every fiber of her being sang with their anger. His mouth gave her no mercy, hot and hard and overwhelming. His fangs pricked her. She bit back, taking his full lower lip between her teeth.

He closed his arm around her waist, locking her against him. Cupping the back of her head in his implacable hand, he tilted her face up and kissed her harder.

This was nothing like the one polite, hapless kiss of her life, which had gotten her into such deep trouble. She was in much greater trouble now.

Her arm stung, but he didn't put his hands anywhere near it. He gripped her buttock and squeezed through her skirts. She braced her hands on his shoulders to push him off of her, but found herself digging her nails into him instead.

When he tore his mouth away, she heaved a breath. "Nora," he said, his voice gravelly. "Offer me your throat again—on the bed this time."

The air filling her lungs restored some coherent thought. She realized she had him right where she wanted him. One more drink of the poison, and he wouldn't have the strength to hold her like this ever again. She pushed him toward the bed, preempting any negotiation with more kisses.

When the back of his knees hit the mattress, triumph glinted in his eyes. "Can you deny you want me under you?"

"I cannot." She could scarcely believe these words were coming out of her mouth. But it was all according to plan, she reminded herself. "I'm offering to ride you while you drink from me."

"This isn't the Drink any longer. This is what we call the Feast." He unfastened his high-collared robe, revealing his own throat. Then the golden-brown contours of his chest and torso, accentuated by black hair. He shrugged the robe off his broad shoulders.

A strange longing filled her as her gaze swept down his muscular arms. She could tell by his strength that he had once been a soldier. But not a scar blemished his immortal body.

He stretched out on the bed, half reclining against the pillows. Her mouth watered, as if she too were a blood-thirsty heretic.

There was no husband in her future. This was the only time she would ever share this bed with anyone. She had this one opportunity to discover what it felt like. And no one would ever know what had happened in this room.

As long as she kept her maidenhead, she wouldn't betray the promise she'd made to herself.

She drew her skirts up, careful to gather plenty of fabric to cushion the scabbard. What a dangerous game she was playing. A rush coursed through her limbs as she climbed onto the bed with him.

She slid her leg over him, straddling his lap. His thighs were hard under hers. She rested her hands on his bare chest for balance, positioning herself. He would not feel the smooth leather strap on the inside of her thigh through this much clothing.

"You may not touch my thighs," she informed him. "I will offer you other places for your hands."

"Will you, now? I cannot wait to find out where."

She reached up and began to remove her veil. His heated gaze tracked each pin she plucked out. No one had ever looked at her like this, as if her every move mesmerized him. She had him in her thrall.

"I'm offering you my hair." She tossed her veil aside and shook out her curls. As she leaned down over him, he reached up to bury both hands in her mane. The feeling of his fingers on her scalp sent a tingle through the rest of her.

"Unlace my gown," she invited.

He didn't tease her like the night before. He tugged open her bodice with demanding hands. "No undergarments tonight? That is clearly an offer."

"Leave my sleeves on," she reminded him.

"Of course." He held his hands out to her. And waited.

Her tongue darted out to wet her lips. No one would ever find out. And she needed to make sure he was thoroughly distracted before she made her move.

She took his hand in hers and pressed it to her belly. She slid his palm down her skin, past the vee of her open gown. When his fingers touched her nether curls, she sucked in a breath.

"When you offered me your hair," he said, "I had no idea you would be so generous."

"Touch me here," she said. "Any way you like."

"Oh, Nora, are you sure you can withstand the temptation if I show you this?"

"Yes," she snarled.

He gave her that presumptuous smile of his. "Has anyone touched you here before?"

"Of course not."

"Have you ever touched yourself?"

That bastard. She didn't answer, but she felt her cheeks flaming, and his smile widened.

"Show me how you like to be touched," he said.

She guided his hand between her legs. A frisson traveled through her at the feeling of his big, strong hand cupping her. Together, they pressed their fingers into her folds.

"You're already wet," he purred. "It was a good kiss, wasn't it? But it left you wanting more."

She dipped his finger into her core, then slicked her most sensitive place. He followed her lead, letting her move his finger in a circle around the bud of nerves.

She bit down hard on her lip. His hand felt so different...so good...

"Is this how you like it?" he asked.

She nodded, her hair falling in her eyes. She kept her hand on his for a moment longer, but he soon had the rhythm. When her grip went slack, he took over. He didn't need her to show him anything. He knew exactly how to touch her.

"You can't read my mind!" she protested again.

"But I can sense what gives you pleasure…and I have five hundred years of experience with the female body."

She gasped, bracing her hands on his chest for support.

Wrapping her hair around his other hand, he pulled her closer. He kissed his way roughly down her throat, his caresses a smooth torture between her legs. "One release is never enough for you, is it?"

She swiveled her hips into the rhythm of his touch, chasing the sensations.

"Do you have to pleasure yourself over and over to feel satisfied?"

He *could* sense her darkest desires. He increased the pressure of his fingers. She sank into his touch, her thighs trembling as he built the delicious tension inside her. Her body responded to his dexterous hand with such greed that she could feel herself crashing toward release already.

He eased off, leaving her quivering on the edge. "Is it hard to be quiet when you climax?"

She bit his shoulder to keep from moaning.

"I've covered your room in veil spells. I'm going to make you scream for me tonight, and no one will hear you."

"I'm not that depraved," she rasped.

"There is nothing depraved about your appetites. You need someone as hungry as you are to enjoy them with you."

He struck her throat. Pleasure tore down through her body and flowed up from his hand. His ravenous sucks at her vein and the relentless glide of his fingers crashed together, too intense.

She stifled her scream against his neck. When the first waves had barely eased, he kept drawing on her throat, holding the thread of tension taut inside her. She snapped, and longer, deeper spasms wracked her body, leaving her gasping with relief.

He could make her come apart all night. His wicked power could exorcise her desires.

But the force of his bite weakened. The poison was working.

His grip on her hair slipped, and his other hand slid out of her gown. Cold struck her throat as his jaw went slack. It was already over.

It was time for her to act.

"Nora?" he wavered.

That plea pulled at her heart.

She eased his head back on the pillow. Her pulse raced with a panic she had never expected. All she could think was that no one had ever showed a shred of respect for her foolish drawings except this Hesperine.

Lies. All of it. This illusion of closeness meant nothing. His seduction would only lead to her paying for his brother's death for all eternity.

Nora reached under her skirts and slid the blade along her thigh.

When she raised Arceo, his eyes widened, and he tried to lift his hands. But she held him down easily. Who was the helpless one now?

A scream of rage tore out of her as she brought the blade down.

FIVE

The Forgotten Martyr

D AV WATCHED THE BLADE COME down, his immortal body powerless to stop her. Nora's outcry echoed through the Blood Union, a lifetime of anguish lashing out in one act of fury.

Dav's magic roared from him in answer. That flash of power revealed the truth. He was the target of her blade, but not her anger.

He seized the magic her pain had summoned to life, and his Will to survive bent his reborn power to his command. He spun his theramancy deep into her thoughts.

Her memories flared in his mind's eye, like lightning strikes that overlay the present. Her parents' faces. A bloodied knife. Then firelight glinting along the oncoming blade in her hand.

She gasped, her thoughts shying from his presence in her mind. Her aim moved an inch.

The dagger plunged into his chest. Light exploded behind his eyelids, and his magic shattered out of his grasp.

Agony coursed through his veins. He couldn't see or hear. Couldn't breathe.

Goddess, let the pain end.

No. No, I am not ready to die.

He didn't know how long it was before his vision cleared. He could still see the canopy of Nora's bed over him. Her heart beat nearby. And in his chest, his own heart labored on.

He stared at the dagger protruding from his chest. He recognized the gold hilt encrusted with topaz. He had seen it in his brother's memories as Rahim's life had slipped away. This weapon had sent Rahim retreating to Orthros, unable to heal himself, barely able to step. By the time he had made it home, it had been too late.

Dav was on borrowed time. If only he had managed to heal Nora's mind before now. He had been trying all night, struggling to remaster his power. Why had his mind healing chosen the hour of his death to come to her aid?

Dav would not survive this night. But there was still time to make his and Rahim's deaths mean something. Dav could still save Nora.

She huddled on the foot of the bed, her face hidden by the curtain of her hair. A streak of blood soaked through her sleeve. "The dagger was supposed to protect me from your magic."

He coaxed some air into his lungs. "It would, if I were a mind mage. But I'm a mind healer."

As he spoke, he eased his magic deeper. She clutched her head. She didn't even know she had been harmed. Her tormentor had robbed her of the power to choose healing. Dav would restore her Will to her.

"Nora, look at me."

She raised her head, her eyes wide. "What are you doing to me?"

"I'll heal the injury inside your mind that has warped your memories, so you'll understand what really happened the night your parents died."

"Why should I believe anything you say?"

Her reality was altering before her eyes. What evidence could he possibly give her when she didn't know who to believe? Through his pain, the words of a greater Hesperine than he came to mind, and he gave Nora the wisdom of Queen Soteira. "'Questioning is not a betrayal of the truth. It is the only way to prove your truth to yourself. To be a heretic is to question everything.'"

"I'm not a heretic!"

"Look into your memories and tell me if you are not."

The scars in her mind twisted Dav's magic into unnatural shapes. Her anguish became his own. There was too much for him to heal before he died. He could not undo a lifetime of abuse in one night. But he could set her on the path toward healing.

"Does it hurt?" he asked her.

"N-no," she gasped.

A smile came to his face. "How does it feel to have me this close?"

She wrapped her arms around herself. "Safe."

He traced farther along the scars. All their pathways led to the crisis in the center of her mind. As he neared her misshapen memories, tears slipped down her cheeks.

He flexed his hand. "Come here, Nora."

She shook her head.

He touched the deep wound with the first delicate thread of theramancy. She moaned.

"You're going to be all right," he reassured her.

His magic came to hand, precise and masterful. In his dying moments, he performed the most challenging healing of his career. As he reordered disjointed pieces of her life into complete experiences, he became lost in her, and nothing else seemed to matter.

He rebuilt her mind's Sanctuary, a bastion against her other scars. Her memories of that night flared to life again, and they relived them together.

❧❧

Nora knelt before *the shrine of Andragathos. She heard the dagger case open.*

"You let him kiss you," came Sir Virtus's voice. "Of all your transgressions, this is the most shocking. I thought better of you, especially after the many times I have purified you."

"He kissed me first."

"What did you do to tempt him? Did you smile at him? Perhaps you let some of your hair escape your veil?"

"No! It wasn't my fault."

"It is always your fault. It amazes me that you can get a kiss out of a man, but not a marriage proposal."

His footsteps approached. Nora covered her scarred arms with her hands.

His tone of reassurance sent a shiver down her spine. "For the sake of the Order's reputation, I will silence the gossip. And I will never abandon you, no matter how much you shame yourself. I will keep helping you become your better self."

Sir Virtus loomed over her, Sancti in his hand. But this time, he held Arceo, too.

All she could do now was take her punishment with grace. He drew Sancti's edge along one of her scars to reopen it. Hot, bright magic sliced into her. He gave her other arm the same treatment, and blood trickled down to her elbow, burning her skin.

"This will be your deepest purification of all," he said.

Pain tore through her shoulder, and sunfire burst behind her eyelids. Through the glare, she stared in shock at Sancti embedded in her flesh.

The door of the shrine swung open. Her mother sailed in, all righteous fury. Her father charged forward with his hand on his sword. "What in our god's name are you doing?"

Sir Virtus and her parents shouted at each other over Nora's head, their words swimming together in her roaring ears. Then Sir Virtus raised his arm. With a flick of his fingers, he threw the Blade of Protection.

Nora could do nothing but watch it fly and land in her father's heart. He crumpled, his sword clattering on the floor. Her mother screamed and went down on her knees, throwing herself over his body.

Nora yanked Sancti out of her shoulder and made a wild swing at Sir Virtus. His grip crushed her wrist. He wrested the dagger from her hand and threw again. The Blade of Purification cut through the air and plunged into her mother's back. Her weeping fell silent.

Nora found her feet and backed away from Sir Virtus. "What have you done?"

His rage drained away, and his face went slack with shock. He came toward her, his hands out. "I can still save you. Come here, and Sancti will erase this terrible memory from your mind. I will be your father now that your parents are gone."

She raced for the door and fled down the corridor, clutching her injured shoulder.

"No!" His heavy footfalls chased her. "I cannot lose you. I will not fail you."

She lost him in the fortress's twisting passageways and found her way out through a postern. With no thought of where she was headed, she tripped and scrambled through the dark woods. When she came out into the clearing, she hid behind the boulder to heave air into her burning lungs. But her head swam, and blood kept dripping onto the ground in front of her. Her vision began to darken.

She came to with her head resting on someone's lap, his hand pressed to her wound. Gentle magic washed through her, a buffer between her and the pain. She looked up into the kind face of her rescuer.

"I'm Rahim," he said. "What's your name?"

"Nora."

"Don't be afraid, Nora." He smiled, and she saw his fangs.

But she wasn't afraid of the Hesperine. His fangs were far less threatening than the daggers in Sir Virtus's hands.

"I'm a healer," Rahim explained. "This wound was dealt by an artifact, so it will take me some time to mend."

"He's coming for me! Please…we must escape."

"Your body can't withstand magical transport until I heal you."

"We'll have to run. He's a holy knight. He wants me alive— but he'll kill you."

"*You won't get far while losing this much blood. I'll stop the bleeding as quickly as I can and hope my veil spells hold against him.*"

As she fought for consciousness, he kept talking to her, his voice so steady and reassuring. He told her of where he could take her for safety, spinning visions of the Hesperine homeland in her mind.

"*We can give you Sanctuary,*" *Rahim promised.*

"*He'll keep me with him at any cost. He can find me anywhere in Tenebra.*"

"*But not in Orthros. We can give you a new life.*"

"*Why?*" *she rasped.* "*My family has killed so many of your kind. Why would you do this for me?*"

"*None of this is your fault.*"

In all her life, no one had ever said that to her before.

She looked down at Rahim's fingers, covered in her blood. He held her life in his hands. And he was trying to give it back to her, although a Knight of Andragathos could attack at any moment.

"*Please,*" *Nora wept,* "*give me Sanctuary.*"

"*That is a sacred request. I will get you to safety behind the Queens' ward, or die trying.*" *Suddenly, he cocked his head.* "*I hear the knight. He's combing the woods for you. Come on. We can make it to the nearest Hesperine refuge.*"

Rahim lifted her in his arms. Now she too could hear Sir Virtus's heavy boots crashing through the woods.

"*Don't try to hide from me, Nora!*" *he shouted.* "*Sancti calls to your wounds. I can sense where you are.*"

The ground fell away as Rahim levitated. The clearing swept past at breathtaking speed.

"*Nothing can hide from the Blade of Purification.*" *Sir Virtus called.* "*It cuts through lies—and Hesperine veil spells.*"

Something whistled past them. Rahim jerked against her. The magic buoying them disappeared, and they crashed to the ground, tumbling down the hillside. Nora crawled toward Rahim, spotting the Blade of Purification out of reach in the grass. His arm bled where Sancti had clipped him.

Sir Virtus burst from the trees. Nora threw herself toward Rahim, but her wounded body was too slow. Arceo grazed her cheek and plunged into his heart.

"No!" She closed her fingers around the hilt.

Rahim wrapped his hand around hers. "I must—return to Orthros. For healing from the Queen. No use to you dead. In Hespera's name, I swear I will come back for you and free you from him."

"I believe you."

Together, they pulled the dagger out of his chest. Rahim disappeared before her eyes.

Nora rounded on Sir Virtus, Arceo in her hand. Dodging her attack, he lunged past her and snatched up Sancti. He blocked her next swing with his blade.

She had no hope of besting a knight in single combat. Within moments, he had disarmed her and forced her to the ground. "We'll make this awful night disappear, my dear. I will take good care of you."

He drove Sancti into the wound Rahim had tried to heal.

Nora surfaced from her memories with a gasp. She lay against Dav, her face pressed to his chest. Eye to eye with the topaz in Arceo's hilt.

"No." She sat up, her hands hovering uselessly over the dagger. "What have I done?"

"Listen to me. You can still escape Virtus. I'll tell you how to find the tower. Make a libation…ask for Sanctuary…the magic will open to you."

"I'm not leaving you! Help me understand what you need." She drew a deep breath, gathering her calm. "If I remove the dagger, you'll bleed. Which is worse—Arceo's magic, or the blood loss?"

"Save yourself. That's enough for me."

"No. There must be a way to heal you. If you drink pure human blood, will it purge Arceo's magic from you?"

Dav moved very carefully, covering her hand with his. "That didn't save Rahim. Not even our Queen's magic could heal him."

"Even if all my blood can give you is comfort, I will shed it for you."

She scrambled off the bed and went to the wall, where she pressed the stone that opened a hidden niche. She rifled through the secrets she kept from Sir Virtus and seized the two vials she had stolen from the shrine chamber.

The white bottle of poison was chained to the gold bottle that held the antidote, in case a knight needed to revive a Hesperine prisoner. Nora uncapped the cure and tossed back its contents. She counted to fourteen, time slipping through her fingers while she waited for the potion to work.

When warmth shot through her body, she raced back to Dav's side. She tore out of her festival gown and climbed onto the bed. "I'll remove the dagger now, and then I want you to drink from me."

"Please, Nora. Go."

"I will not abandon you," she swore. "Just like you and Rahim never gave up on me."

Dav swallowed. "If your blood…is the last thing I taste… then I'll keep fighting, too."

"On the count of three. One." She took hold of the dagger. "Two." She held her gown ready to staunch the blood. "Three."

She pulled the blade out, his shout of pain ringing in her ears. Hurling the dagger away, she pressed her gown to the wound. His blood soaked the gold and white fabric.

She pressed her throat to his mouth. "Drink!"

His fangs shot out, and he sank them into her neck with feral force. She pressed her fist to his wound, breathing hard as he tore her blood out of her. He groaned against her skin, and she felt his magic reaching for her mind again.

"Yes," she said. "I'm here. You're not alone."

His power wove into her, hers into him. In that moment, she felt closer to him than she ever had to a living soul. And she was losing him.

His blood soaked through the gown onto her hand. Her tears splashed onto his chest. She would do anything to go back and change even one of her choices.

She held his head, fearing the moment when his bite would weaken and he would slip away.

She would hold on to him for as long as she could.

SIX

Unholy Confessions

SUDDENLY NORA FELT DAV'S FINGERS clamp around the back of her neck. With his other hand, he shoved the gown away and flattened her bloody palm over his heart.

The wound had closed. She didn't understand why or how. She only knew that her blood was healing him.

"Yes," she cried, "take everything you need."

In a burst of speed, he flipped her onto her back, and his weight came down upon her. She clutched him between her thighs and ran her hand over his body, feeling the new life in him. Her own body pounded with awareness of everywhere they touched, as if she too were coming back to life.

He slid her hand down the damp planes of his stomach to the front of his trousers. She felt the silk fabric and the forbidden steel beneath. Together, they rid him of the last barrier of clothing between them. Admonitions from the Order's matrons fled from her mind. Her thoughts filled with words she was not supposed to know and acts she was not supposed to imagine.

She gave in to her desire to explore his cock. He wrapped her hand around his shaft and guided her strokes up and down. Fascinated, she learned his shape and texture. His jaw clenched, deepening his bite, and they moaned together.

But his canines eased out of her neck, her hips twitching with the sensation. He gave the wounds on her throat worshipful licks until they healed into raw new skin. She arched under him, feeling empty, but he held her down and lifted his head.

"Nora. Are you really offering me everything?"

"If you'll have me."

"I'll have you in every way you can imagine, on one condition."

"Name your price."

"You will not feel an ounce of shame about what we do to each other in this bed tonight."

The guilt had bled out of her a little more with his every bite, leaving behind this wild rush in her veins. "You can touch me anywhere you wish. On one condition."

His tongue swept across his stained lips for another taste of her blood. "Anywhere?"

"Nowhere is forbidden."

"I'll promise you anything."

"I don't want some tasteful consummation," she demanded. "Don't bed me like a proper husband. Ravish me like a heretic."

He ran his hand up her thigh, over the impressions the scabbard had left on her flesh, and squeezed.

She held his glowing gaze and let the heat in his eyes burn her. His magic swept deeper into her mind, a dark thrill.

He was upon her with Hesperine swiftness and grace. In one heartbeat, his hard length was buried inside her. She dragged in a hoarse gasp, pinned to the bed on his shaft, her core stretched around him.

"Did it hurt?" he whispered.

"No," she moaned. "It's too good."

He pulled out with blinding speed, leaving her wet and reeling. And then he filled her again, driving inside her with the power of an immortal.

In the ancestral bed of generations of holy knights, Nora lay impaled beneath a Hesperine and spread her legs wider.

Dav kissed her, shocking in his tenderness. "I love how wide your mouth is." He smoothed her hair back from her face. "I love how wild your curls are." He arched his back, and the different angle of his body pressed new pleasure into her. His warm breath washed over her chest. "And *Goddess*, I love the size of your breasts."

He closed his mouth over her nipple and sucked. Clutching his shoulders, she squirmed under his implacable hips. He worked her breasts over with his mouth, first one, then the other, until she was on the verge of climax and begging him.

But then he lifted his mouth away. He turned his head. When he kissed the scar Sancti had left on her shoulder, she froze under him.

He waited a moment, then licked the cut on her arm. "Does it hurt?"

She swallowed hard. "Not now."

He lapped at the sluggishly bleeding wound. She could feel the sweet darkness of Hesperine magic flowing into her, putting out the burning light. Tears slipped down her cheeks.

When only unbroken skin remained under his tongue, he lifted his head and recaptured her gaze. He began to move inside her, his forceful rhythm grinding her thoughts down into a haze. She braced her feet on the bed, needing leverage. Needing to move. She rocked her hips up for his thrusts.

"I love how greedy you are," he said.

Faster, harder, he pounded into her. She urged him on in wordless groans.

"I love the sounds you make," he snarled.

She cried out, half growling, as her core convulsed around his shaft. His fangs drove into her throat once more, releasing her blood. She writhed under his bite, wringing out her long years of hunger on his cock. She felt him shudder with her and pulse against her inner walls.

At last she lay back, his fangs still embedded in her throat, knowing he had spilled a Hesperine's fruitless seed inside her. She was thoroughly corrupted, and it felt better than anything she had imagined. She let out a wild laugh.

He put his mouth to her ear. "You want more, don't you?"

"I'm so hungry, Dav."

By the predawn hours, she lay spooned against him, finally too spent to move. The deepest ease she had ever known settled into her languid limbs. But her body's reprieve was not enough to keep her thoughts at bay.

She said the words she needed to say. "I'm so sorry about Rahim."

"I'm so sorry about your parents," Dav said. "In Orthros,

when someone loses a loved one, we say, 'Your grief runs in my veins.'"

She turned her head, looking at his shadowed face in the dying firelight. "Your grief runs in my veins, Dav."

He stroked her scars. "I know it does."

"Why did he come here? Why would he do all of that for me?"

"It is an honored practice among our people. He became a Hesperine errant—an immortal who leaves Orthros to travel human lands, offering aid to your people. He was moved to use our great power to alleviate suffering in the mortal world."

"And when he couldn't come back for me…you did."

"It was his last wish. He begged me to rescue you. I hope you can forgive me for taking half a year to accept that calling, and not so gracefully."

She pressed her eyes shut. "If you can forgive me for greeting you as an enemy."

His hand stilled on her arm. "That was not your doing. Nora, I will not let Sir Virtus hurt you again."

The dream Rahim had given her that night came back to life. It was possible. A new life.

"Forget this place." Dav whispered the greatest seduction of all in her ear. "Leave Tenebra behind. Come home to Orthros with me and let every night be like this one."

She wrapped his arm around her, pressing back into him. Allowing herself one more moment of astonishing comfort from this being she had not known three days ago.

"Can you forgive me if I stay?" she asked.

His arm tightened around her. "Why in Hespera's name would you stay?"

"You are trying to honor Rahim's memory," she said, "but I must honor my parents. I can only think of one way to do both. I must become a dame in the Order so I can hold Castra Gloria—and work from within to protect Hesperines from the knights."

"The Order doesn't matter," he ground out. "I need you to come back to Orthros with me."

"It matters to me. It mattered to my parents."

"Nora." So much pain in one word.

"I'm so sorry." Her voice thickened. "I cannot fulfill Rahim's wish. But we can get justice for him and my parents. I have a plan. Will you come back tomorrow night so we can end Sir Virtus—together?"

Dav pushed her onto her back. His golden eyes glowed at her through the darkness. "Here are my terms. I will go along with your plan. But when we have defeated him, you will give me one more chance to change your mind."

She should refuse. If he tried to convince her again, she might lose the will to refuse him.

But she wanted one more night of a Hesperine's persuasion, before she must remember how to be dutiful.

"I accept your terms."

❦

Dav followed Nora down the corridor, the most dangerous shadow in the dark hallway. Her blood flowed in his cleansed veins. Last night had changed him, as profoundly as the night he had transformed from human to Hesperine.

There was only one possible explanation for why she had

been able to save him. She was the mate whose blood could free him from hunger for any other. The partner destined to share his long eternity.

Nora was his Grace.

Dav had already drunk more than enough from her to awaken their bond—and the Craving, the addiction every Graced Hesperine suffered. If she wouldn't accept Sanctuary, he would face a short future of withdrawal and starvation.

He had found her at last, after all these centuries alone. His brother had died bringing them together.

Dav would not let anyone take her from him.

As she approached the door of the shrine where Sir Virtus awaited her, her terror washed over the Blood Union. But she put one foot in front of the other, walking with determination toward her greatest fear.

Hidden in veil spells, Dav looked Sir Virtus in the eye. Here was the fanatic who had tormented her. His were the hands that had killed Rahim.

Dav's hand tightened on Arceo's hilt. He could no longer call himself a healer after what he was about to do. He didn't know what that made him. He only knew Sir Virtus was the greater monster.

"Honora," came the man's warning tone, "Arceo has not been returned, and now three more relics are missing."

"I know, Uncle. I noticed when I was saying my afternoon prayers. I have spent all evening questioning the servants." She held out the scabbard. "I found this."

Sir Virtus snatched the empty dagger sheath from her. "Where was it?"

"Someone left it on my father's tomb."

Dav enjoyed watching the color drain from Sir Virtus's face.

"Who?" the knight demanded.

"I do not know, Uncle. But it was very painful for me to visit the crypt today. Will you help me find comfort in prayer?"

"Of course, child. Of course."

Sir Virtus took Nora's arm, and her emotions flinched. Dav bared his fangs. He stalked behind them as they walked down the central aisle of the shrine.

The auras of the relics stung his arcane senses. The whole chamber was aglow with bright halos of anti-Hesperine magic. Nora had rid the room of the three artifacts that could reveal his presence, but he was still surrounded by things that could destroy him if he made one wrong move.

Dav hated watching Nora kneel with that man before the emblem of her judgmental god. This heretic would enjoy desecrating Andragathos's shrine.

Nora's voice disrupted the quiet of the room. "On my last night as Lady of Gloria, I have meditated on my duty to my parents. Will you pray for their souls with me, Uncle Virtus?"

A drop of sweat trickled down his brow. "Certainly, daughter."

Sir Virtus bowed his head, closing his eyes, and began to drone a prayer. Nora slid her hand into the folds of her skirts.

This was their chance. Dav moved swiftly to the box Nora had described to him. The lock was a mundane one that whispered open at a touch of his magic. He eased the lid back.

Arceo heated in his hand, and a cold fire answered from the opal in Sancti's white-gold hilt. Pain flared behind Dav's eyes, and his stomach turned over. He wouldn't be able to hold both daggers long.

Gritting his teeth, he closed his hand around Sancti's hilt. The current of magic between the daggers flared along his arms, white hot. He slipped over to Nora, kneeling to press the Blade of Purification into her grasp.

He rested his scorched hand on her shoulder and tapped once. Twice. Three times.

They moved in unison. He heard the blades glide through the air, too quiet for mortal ears. They swung together at the praying man's heart.

Dav's dagger never landed. Glass shattered. Fragrant smoke struck Dav in the face, obscuring his vision and clawing into his lungs.

"Step away!" Nora cried.

Dav transported himself to the other side of the room, his eyes watering and coughs wracking him. Through clouds of smoke, he made out the silhouette of the knight, swinging a sword where his neck had just been.

"Nora?" Dav called. "Are you all right?"

He sensed her aura darting toward him.

The figure of Sir Virtus loomed between them. "Did you think you could bring a Hesperine into the shrine without my knowing? Did you think removing those relics would fool me? My amulet warned me the moment that creature approached."

Nora let out an angry cry. "This is Andragathian Incense! The smoke will reveal y—"

"Silence!" Sir Virtus barked, and Nora gasped. Her pain flared in Dav's senses.

Dav Willed open the door of the shrine. Air swept in from the corridor, and the incense thinned. He saw Nora in Sir Virtus's grip, his sword at her throat.

"How could you betray me like this?" Sir Virtus lamented. "After everything I did to teach you goodness."

Dav calculated options in his mind. If he stepped to Sir Virtus, would the man have time to slit Nora's throat before Dav could stop him?

Sir Virtus dragged Nora toward a pedestal, where an orb of magefire burned in a golden chalice. "You will pay for this, Hesperine. I will drive you from this sacred place with holy fire."

When Nora's hand moved in the folds of her skirts, Dav realized. Sir Virtus had been so preoccupied with the Hesperine threat that he had made his greatest mistake of all.

He had underestimated Nora.

She raised Sancti and slashed the Blade of Purification across Sir Virtus's arm. The man drew a hollow gasp.

It was all the diversion Dav needed. He stepped to Nora's side, ancient muscle memory returning to him. He dealt Sir Virtus blow after blow that he had learned in the Imperial army. When the man was disarmed and on his knees, Dav seized him by the throat and hurled him against the Shield of Andragathos. He held the gaping mortal there and let the man struggle against his immortal strength.

Dav smiled, putting his fangs on display. "You're the coward who threw a dagger at a fleeing Hesperine. He was my brother."

The scent of the man's fear filled the shrine.

Nora searched his surcoat, depriving him of his belt

pouch of incense, his amulet, and a hidden prayer book that emanated magic. She tossed the incense into a bowl of healing water and dropped the other two artifacts into the cup of magefire. Nora watched his face while his relics burned.

Sir Virtus moaned. "I can still save you, child."

She laughed loudly. Tearing the veil from her hair, she let her red mane free. "You failed, 'Uncle' Virtus."

"Turn away from this creature! We can defeat him together."

Nora held Sancti's tip to Sir Virtus's throat. "It's too late. He's bitten me. I gave him my blood over and over again. Then I welcomed him into my bed. And I enjoyed it."

Sir Virtus spat prayers and curses at them.

"Don't shout about holiness to me," Nora shot back. "You killed my parents."

Specters of guilt haunted Sir Virtus's aura. "This Hesperine has addled your mind! Lies!"

"I remember everything," she said.

Bitterness welled out of the man, a bile so potent, it must have been festering in him for years. "I was always a better knight. A better man. I gave the Order my all. I even resisted my lust for your mother. Only for your father to take her to wife instead. And what thanks did I get from the Order for my self denial? They celebrated him. They entrusted all the greatest relics to him."

"When he was given Arceo," Nora said, "that was the final blow, wasn't it? You were planning to take both daggers for yourself."

"I was their rightful wielder! He couldn't even discipline his own daughter properly! He was too fastidious to use

Sancti on you. Why do you think he asked me to do it every time? I was a better father to you than he ever was. Your mother understood what was necessary. She prayed for your soul whenever she bandaged your wounds."

Dav's thoughts reeled. But his own shock was not mirrored in Nora's aura. This was a memory she had never lost.

Dav searched her face. "Your parents *knew*?"

Nora took a step back. "I was always a disappointment."

"They allowed him to do that to you?"

"It wasn't their fault. Sir Virtus must have persuaded them it was necessary."

"They asked it of him!"

"They were trying to help me."

"The night they died," Dav said, "they didn't come here to rescue you."

Nora clutched her arm, Sancti dangling from her other hand. "They were coming to join him. But then Father saw that Sir Virtus had taken Arceo. He was angry about the theft of the relic."

Her parents had cared more for this dagger than their daughter. Even as Dav's hand tightened around Sir Virtus's throat, he knew Nora's first enemies were already dead. And they had left her with scars so deep, she could not even bring herself to acknowledge that what they'd done was wrong.

Dav fingered Arceo's hilt in his free hand. All of Hespera's sacred tenets faded from his mind under the red haze of his rage and grief. He wanted to drive the blade into Sir Virtus's heart. Once for Rahim. Again for Nora. Over and over for all the blows he could not deal her parents.

While Dav had been writing research treatises in the

placid halls of Orthros, Nora had been here. Every day of her life had brought suffering. When Dav had begged his brother not to waste his power on ungrateful mortals, Rahim had come here. He had risked everything to save this one life.

It took all of Dav's Will not to tear Sir Virtus apart with the dagger. But the memory of his brother's gentle aura stayed his hand.

Vengeance was not a word his brother had known, nor a word Queen Soteira had taught Dav.

Revenge was different from justice.

Dav swung the dagger with all his immortal might. He listened to Sir Virtus scream and heard the blade point crack the shield. He left the man pinned to the shrine, Arceo embedded in his shoulder, his heart still beating.

Nora stared at Dav. "Don't you want your revenge?"

"I didn't come here for that. I came for you. What do you want?"

She spun toward Sir Virtus, her knuckles white on Sancti's hilt. "I want him to know how I felt."

At last, her anger and her dagger were aimed at the same target. The whites of Sir Virtus's eyes showed as he watched his judgment approach.

Nora plunged the Blade of Purification into Sir Virtus's other shoulder. The magic of the two daggers collided in a glare of light. Memories flared across the surface of his thoughts, coming to Dav in glimpses. Nora's parents, falling dead. Nora, weeping, begging him for compassion. He began to sob, muttering confessions.

Nora staggered back. "What's happening? Sancti never did this to me."

"It must be the combined magic of both daggers. His own transgressions are flashing before his eyes, over and over." Dav mustered his power to shut out Sir Virtus's thoughts.

With his senses clear, he heard the heavy footfalls in the corridors and the voices of men rising through the fortress. He slammed the door shut with his Will.

"Dav, what is it?" Nora asked.

"A large party of warriors is approaching the shrine."

Nora swore. "The other knights have arrived."

"What will they do with him if they find him like this?"

Nora's lip curled. "The Grand Master will hear his confessions and strip away everything he ever worked for in the Order."

"That sounds like justice to me."

The voices drew nearer. Nora hesitated.

"They can't find us here," Dav said.

Her eyes beseeched him. "You know you must bring me back."

"You promised me one more chance to change your mind."

She came into his arms, and he stepped her away to the tower. The quiet of the Hesperine Sanctuary wrapped around them.

But her aura was in chaos. He heard echoes of her parents' words in her thoughts. *Disappointed... Ashamed... Too loud. Too buxom. Wish you'd been a son.*

Nora pulled Dav's mouth down to hers and kissed him fiercely. He let her silence her own thoughts against his lips. His magic and his blood stirred in instinctive response to her need. But he only held her gently, waiting until she came up for air.

Seduction was not how he would try to change her mind this time. He would offer her something even more tempting. The truth.

"Remember what Rahim said to you. None of this is your fault."

Her hands closed on the front of his robe.

"What your parents did to you was wrong," Dav said. "It will take time for you to feel the truth of this. That's natural, after they played mind games with you for years and wore you down. Which is why you need to surround yourself with voices who will tell you the truth about yourself."

She hid her tears against his chest.

He lifted her face in both hands, stroking her. "You're perfect, Nora. Everything about you. Just as you are."

The new thoughts spinning through her pulled at the scars in her mind. "What was it your queen said? Questioning is not a betrayal of the truth?"

"It is the only way to prove your truth to yourself."

"I don't know what my truth is yet. But I…I am questioning. Everything."

Dav rested his forehead on hers. "I want to be at your side while you question. Will you let me do that?"

"Dames of the Order are not permitted to question anything."

"But heretics are."

"If I never return, the castle will fall down."

"And you can build your own."

The light of possibilities rose in her aura. The Blood Union ached with her longing. She was so close to changing her mind.

Dav was done choosing the safe path. He took the most dangerous gamble of his existence and put his life in her hands one more time. "And if you need another reason… you should know why your blood healed me."

Nora's brow furrowed. "I do want to understand how that was possible."

"For every Hesperine, there is one person whose blood is more potent than any other. The perfect elixir, which can sustain them for eternity. No other blood could have been restorative enough to pull me back from the brink of death."

"How? What magic is this?"

"It is a bond fated in our blood. We call it Grace. And now that I have tasted you, my Grace, I will die without your blood."

She put a hand to her throat, where the unseen mark of his bite lingered. "It simply…is? Naturally, without any effort? *My* blood can do that?"

"You're perfect," he said again.

A sense of power welled up in her, drowning out the doubts in her emotions. "It seems I have you at a disadvantage, Dav. You need me. What does that mean for my future if I return with you to Orthros?"

He pulled her hand away and scraped her vein with his teeth to feel her shiver. "It means you are my mate, and the only person I will ravish like a heretic for the rest of eternity."

Her throat moved as she swallowed. "Eternity is a long time."

"It will take you time to feel the truth of this too, I know. But I've been hoping to find my Grace for five hundred years. I can wait as long as you need to embrace the idea. I will be patient while you design your own palaces, until you decide you'd like to build something with me."

Nora wrapped her arms around him.

"Can you deny you want what I've shown you?" Dav asked.

"Leave," she demanded. "Never set foot within sight of Castra Gloria again. And take me with you."

Eternal Heresy

Four Years Later

FROM THE ROOFTOP GARDEN AT the peak of the city, Dav stood with Nora and looked out over the domes of Orthros. Polar night draped the sky in indigo, and fresh snow glittered on the many-colored mosaics. He had seen this view for five centuries, but every time she beheld it, he felt like he was looking at the world and at her for the first time.

Dav would never stop wishing Rahim could stand here with them now. But his memory would live forever, and so would Nora.

Dav caressed the thin braid of his hair she wore in her curls. Her vibrant red braid draped down his cheek and over his shoulder, a constant reminder to him and all their people of their Grace bond. The wind tugged at her sleeveless red robe, and Dav ran his hands down her bare arms, caressing her smooth skin. She beamed at him over her shoulder, her fangs tempting him to kiss her.

"You can see it from here! Look." She pointed at one small dome among the others. Dav recognized the top of the Shrine of Hespera that Nora had designed and built to complete her studies with Yasamin.

"Just think," he said, "your contribution to the architecture of Orthros will be seen by everyone who sets foot here in the Queens' garden, for centuries to come."

"Do you think anyone will mind if the kiss I'm about to give you will be seen by everyone?"

"The Queens kiss each other up here all the time." Dav lowered his face toward her.

Nora wrapped her arms around his neck and pressed ardent kisses to his mouth, her fangs teasing his lips. How he enjoyed it every time her new Hesperine appetites overtook her. He heard the last group of Hesperine petitioners depart, but didn't bother to veil himself and Nora. No one begrudged two newly avowed Graces a display of affection.

Dav spoke in her mind, their Grace Union carrying his words directly between their thoughts. *We should go to your shrine later. Alone. I want to perform one of Hespera's most sacred rituals.* He sent her a mental image of her kneeling in the Sanctuary she had built. Then him down on his knees behind her, thrusting inside her while he took her vein.

Nora drew back, pressing her hands to her cheeks. "You indecent Hesperine. I can't appear before the Queens with my face all red."

He gave her an unrepentant grin. "I think they're ready to see us now."

"I'll make you pay for this blush later."

"I look forward to whatever revenge you have in mind."

Hand in hand, they approached the Queens through the garden of white roses. Queen Alea, once from Tenebra and pale like the blooms, sat with Queen Soteira, their Imperial monarch, who was as dark and beautiful as the Goddess's night sky. Their only thrones were their silk cushions. For crowns, they wore one another's Grace braids. Their power was self-evident in the ageless, endless magic in their auras. Dav and Nora put their hands on their hearts and bowed.

Queen Soteira gave them an affectionate smile. "Congratulations on the completion of your studies, Nora. We would be pleased to attend the dedication ceremony for your shrine."

"You honor me, Annassa," she replied, using the Queens' honorific. "Surely you didn't ask to see us only to show me such recognition."

"No," Queen Alea said with a kind laugh. "We would also like to recommend you to someone for your first commission."

"He'll be joining us in a moment," said Queen Soteira.

"Annassa, this is a dream come true." Nora's happiness lit up their Grace Union.

Dav smiled at his mentor. "You have our gratitude."

"He has a position available for a mind healer, as well," Queen Soteira said. "I think you two are just the pair he needs."

The heavy tread of riding boots ascended the steps behind Dav and Nora. They turned to see a Hesperine approaching, dressed not in the silk robes of Orthros, but Tenebran battle gear. The blood-red braid trailing to his ankles was legendary, his grim, hawkish face known to every Hesperine, although seldom seen at home these days. He was one of the most infamous Hesperines errant to ever challenge his people's persecutors.

The First Prince of Orthros had returned.

Dav gave the heart bow, Nora following his lead.

"Firstblood Daryavesh," said the prince. "I hear you are a mind healer after my own heart."

"That is high praise, First Prince." Despite how powerful Dav was, he found himself in awe of the magic pouring off the prince. The Queens' eldest son had inherited Annassa Soteira's dual affinity for mind healing and physical healing.

"I remember your brother as well." A shadow passed over the prince's aura. "He was an admirable healer. Your grief runs in my veins."

The condolence had seldom been more true. The prince had also lost someone he had loved as a brother. Like Rahim, the Hesperine hero Prometheus had sacrificed his life as a Hesperine errant.

"All of Orthros mourns with you," said Dav.

"I prefer action to mourning," the prince replied. "Imagine if there were a Sanctuary in Tenebra where a force of Hesperines errant remained every night of the year. A refuge closer than Orthros, where any of our people could get to our healers right away."

Dav's chest ached. "Such a place might have saved Rahim's life."

The prince gave a tight nod. "I intend to establish a stronghold in enemy territory. I am gathering a force of Hesperines errant to serve there under my command."

"You intend to remain in Tenebra permanently?" Dav asked, astonished.

"With heavy hearts," said Queen Soteira, "we have given him our blessing."

"First Prince," Nora spoke up, "for that many Hesperines to reside in Tenebra permanently is unprecedented. You will live under constant threat of discovery and destruction."

"Which is why I need a fortress, Firstgrace Daryaveshi," the prince replied.

Nora's eyes widened. "You want me to build you a castle?"

"It must pass for a Tenebran lord's castra on the outside." He looked around. "On the inside, it must feel like home."

"And it must be built to withstand the Knights of Andragathos, war mages, necromancer assassins…" As Nora named off Hesperines' many enemies, Dav could already see diagrams taking shape in her mind.

He rested a hand on her arm. "Are you sure you wish to return to Tenebra? Do you feel ready to face it?"

She bit her lip. "And what about you, Dav? Your research, your patients?"

Queen Soteira raised a brow. "Don't think I haven't noticed how restless he's been in his work the past four years."

"I need mind healers like you," the prince said. "You know how to treat the wounds battle leaves on the mind— and you aren't afraid to take up arms when necessary."

Nora met Dav in their Grace Union. *You never wanted to be a Hesperine errant.*

That was before I met you.

She grasped his hand. "There are more Rahims in need of reinforcement in Tenebra, and more Noras in need of rescue."

"I am ready to heal more difficult wounds, if you are ready to build something more dangerous."

She smiled. "We can retire to do research and build palaces in a future century. We have forever."

Together, they turned to face the prince and the adventures that awaited them.

CRAVING MORE FATED MATES AND fang banging set in Nora and Dav's world? Dive into Vela's epic Blood Grace series, starting with the bestselling fantasy romance *Blood Mercy*. Check it out at vroth.co/mercy or keep reading for a preview!

Blood Mercy

**One human. One immortal. Will their alliance
save the kingdom, or will their forbidden love
be a death sentence?**

When Cassia seeks out a Hesperine, he could end her mortal life in a heartbeat. But she has no fear of his magic or his fangs. She knows the real monster is the human king, her father. If he finds out she's bargaining with his enemy, he'll send her to the executioner.

As a Hesperine diplomat, Lio must negotiate with mortals who hate him. Cassia is different, but politics aren't why she captivates the gentle immortal. He wants more than her blood, and if he can't resist the temptation, he'll provoke the war he's trying to prevent.

Slow-burn, spicy romance meets classic fantasy in the Blood Grace series. Follow fated mates Cassia and Lio through their epic story of forbidden love for a guaranteed series HEA.

Lio and the lady stared at each other over her liege-hound's hackles.

The wind blew past her, and her scent struck him anew. He resisted the urge to flare his nostrils and take another deep whiff of her. He had no desire to resemble her beast.

Her hand drifted under the hound's chin, right below all those teeth, and scratched his smear of red fur. She lowered her gaze to the animal. What better way to show Lio she did not fear him than to look away?

He did not smell a whiff of fear on her. It was her trek through the woods that had made her blood lively in her veins. Her heart beat a fast, undulating rhythm in the night, and he caught himself listening with rapt attention. Never had he heard music like this. Not even in Orthros.

He had the Blood Union and all the power the Gift afforded. She had a Hesperine-eating dog. Perhaps they were not entirely on uneven footing.

"You have nothing to fear from Knight," she informed him. "He only goes after monsters."

Her words could not have surprised Lio more if she had recited the Discourses on Love in perfect Divine Tongue. Lio offered her a tardy bow, a deep one to convey sincere respect. Best to err on the side of caution until he was certain of her rank. Despite her spare appearance, the lady was almost certainly important if someone had gone to the effort and expense of bonding a liegehound to her.

This encounter was simply waiting to become a diplomatic disaster. Hespera help him, he must not make a mess of things. It was not too late to salvage the situation, if the reassurance the lady had just offered was to be heeded: she did not regard Lio as a monster.

"It is a good thing you have such a dangerous protector, Lady." Lio adopted a tone of courtly banter, testing her. "I'm afraid vicious monsters do indeed stalk the grounds tonight, seeking to devour beautiful young maidens."

She took the bait, and he heard her laughter for the first time. That airy peal did not sound natural, but studied and wielded as a defense. She looked up from her hound, a faint smile on her lips. "If I happen upon any such creatures, I shall warn you of what they look like."

Lio bowed again. "Gracious thanks. Knight and I might be called upon to drive them away, to ensure they do not disturb any ladies taking the evening air."

"I appreciate your heroic offer. I am quite adept at dealing with monsters, however."

"I suspect you are. Are you called upon to deal with them often?"

She tilted her head. "Are not we all?"

"At the risk of damaging your confidence in me, I can't say I have a great deal of experience in monster slaying, myself."

"You have not been in Tenebra long."

Lio considered his next words. They sailed farther and farther from the safe waters of banter, which no one ruled. "I hold out hope no monster slaying will be necessary during our stay here."

"Of course. You and your company ride under a different banner than the warriors of this house. You are the sort who would rather solve conflicts with words than swords, are you not?"

"I hope so."

"Then there is a favor you can do for me. No monster slaying required."

He folded his hands behind his back. What could she possibly want of him? What could he possibly do for her—safely? "As you say, I ride under a different banner. But perhaps I may still serve you, Lady. What is it you would ask of me?"

"Answer me a question, nothing more." Her heartbeat

jumped again in her chest, although her expression did not change. She continued smoothly, but the playfulness was gone from her voice. "Are there any among your party who perform the Mercy for the dying?"

He was sure every bit of his astonishment showed on his face. He did not answer right away, more on guard now than he had been when he'd first seen the hound. "I was not aware your people and mine used the same name for that Hesperine rite."

"We do not. I prefer yours."

"Then you are quite unusual among your kind."

"Indeed. I even know the way your people honor the dying does not involve feasting on their flesh…or even drinking their blood."

Lio discarded his assumptions about her then and there. "Then you must know I am hesitant to answer you, lest I implicate any of my companions in practices that are…difficult for most of your people to understand."

"Of course. It is best if we do not name names. I ask only for a yes or a no. Can I persuade you to give me that much? As a deed of chivalry?"

Lio sought answers in the Blood Union. He let it draw him into the russet tendrils of light that were the veins beneath her skin. He barely managed not to gasp.

Suddenly, at last, he was in this moment. Not on the greensward dying with a helpless man. He was in the living current of her blood.

Here was the greatest beauty she possessed—a will to survive unlike any Lio had ever felt. A Will so strong it could only have grown under constant threat.

Here was the reason his people spilled their own blood on behalf of her kind. Why the embassy had walked voluntarily into this den of predators and the Queens had allowed them to do so.

This woman the Goddess had given life must fight for every beat of her heart.

Lio unraveled himself from her, struggling to resist the music under her skin. "If you would have me be your knight champion, Lady, you must condescend to offer me at least some small token of yours."

Her smile did not reach her eyes or her blood. "Of course. You would want a flower to adorn your breast. A trophy to carry onto the field."

"Nay, I would beg of you a treasure that is beyond my power to possess. It is yours to share or withhold. But if you will allow me, I promise I shall carry it with honor…and keep it close." He put a hand over his heart. "Your name, Lady."

Her blood rushed faster. She hesitated. "I thought it was agreed no names should pass our lips."

"To protect those who might be endangered, should their names be known."

"Did you imagine that includes only your own people?"

He bowed his head in concession. Hound or no hound, she was still a woman in Tenebra. And she was still disobeying her king. "Forgive me. A knight intends his lady no harm."

"Only a knight can be trusted," she told him. The hound eyed him, tensing as if to stand. "Het, love," she soothed, and the beast stilled.

Lio met the dog's gaze. "I have no wish to trespass on

my lady's generosity, but could I call myself honorable if I answered such a question, not knowing who asks?"

"Fair," she acknowledged. "Yet you ask a name in exchange for a mere yes or no."

"Not at all. For I shall give you my name as well."

"Unwilling to endanger your comrades, but ready to place yourself on the sacrificial altar?"

He tried not to let her metaphor concern him. "A confidence for a confidence. And if that concerns you so, let me ask you this: to whom might I betray you? What reason have I to reveal your secrets?"

She was silent for a long moment, and he began to think he had lost his gamble, and she would turn and leave. But at last she nodded. "Very well. Who offers himself as my champion tonight?"

"Deukalion Komnenos. But my lady must call me Lio, as my friends do."

"A pleasure to meet you…Lio. I am Cassia."

"Cassia." He smiled at her, remembering just in time to keep his lips shut. She was her name, through and through: a spice beloved among Hesperines for its fragrance and flavor. Bitter, unless sweetened.

"May I have the answer to my question, Lio?"

"The answer is no. None of us perform the Mercy. We enter Tenebra to fulfill other duties."

A sigh escaped her, whether of relief or disappointment, the Blood Union did not tell him. And that, he wondered at. For all he beheld in her, there was a great deal he could not discern.

She dipped her head in a deep nod. "Thank you."

He bowed again instead of asking her more questions. Nor did he offer further answers. There was much more he could have told her, of course, but their agreement was only for a yes or no. One did not reveal all one's bargaining power during the first negotiation. He suspected she knew that as well as he did. He had haggled for all she would reveal tonight.

Would he have an opportunity to bargain for more?

Her hand shifted slightly on the dog's head, and he got to his feet. He still watched Lio, but there was no sign of teeth now.

"I bid you good evening." She turned away. "And good meal."

If he had not suspected it already, that last remark convinced him. There was a great deal more about her that would surprise him.

***

Cassia and Lio's saga begins in Blood Grace Book 1, Blood Mercy! Available in ebook, Kindle Unlimited, audio, paperback, hardcover, and special edition at vroth.co/mercy.